## "I don't want you to think I'm trying to get close to you," she clarified.

But no clarification was needed. That wasn't the grip of a woman planning to seduce a man to get him to back off. Or even to soften him up. Her touch was tentative, but the tentativeness didn't make it to her eyes.

She inched even closer. "And this has nothing to do with you being a bad boy."

"Good thing. Because I lost my bad-boy status years ago." Yeah, it was a poor attempt to lighten things up, but since she looked ready to shatter into a thousand little pieces, he thought she could use the levity.

It worked.

The corner of her mouth lifted just a fraction. "I don't think it's a status you can lose. It comes with the looks and the attitude."

He was in trouble here. Yeah, she might not be trying to seduce him, but she was doing it anyway.

Maybe she was right. Once bad, always bad. That was the only explanation Slade could come up with as to why he lowered his head and brushed his mouth over hers.

# RENEGADE GUARDIAN

USA TODAY Bestselling Author

## DELORES FOSSEN

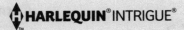

Recycling programs
for this product may
not exist in your area.

ISBN-13: 978-0-373-74778-8

RENEGADE GUARDIAN

Copyright © 2013 by Delores Fossen

All rights reserved. Except for use in any review, the reproduction or utilization of this work in whole or in part in any form by any electronic, mechanical or other means, now known or hereafter invented, including xerography, photocopying and recording, or in any information storage or retrieval system, is forbidden without the written permission of the publisher, Harlequin Enterprises Limited, 225 Duncan Mill Road, Don Mills, Ontario M3B 3K9, Canada.

This is a work of fiction. Names, characters, places and incidents are either the product of the author's imagination or are used fictitiously, and any resemblance to actual persons, living or dead, business establishments, events or locales is entirely coincidental.

This edition published by arrangement with Harlequin Books S.A.

For questions and comments about the quality of this book, please contact us at CustomerService@Harlequin.com.

® and TM are trademarks of Harlequin Enterprises Limited or its corporate affiliates. Trademarks indicated with ® are registered in the United States Patent and Trademark Office, the Canadian Trade Marks Office and in other countries.

Printed in U.S.A.

HARLEQUIN®
www.Harlequin.com

# ABOUT THE AUTHOR

Imagine a family tree that includes Texas cowboys, Choctaw and Cherokee Indians, a Louisiana pirate and a Scottish rebel who battled side by side with William Wallace. With ancestors like that, it's easy to understand why *USA TODAY* bestselling author and former air force captain Delores Fossen feels as if she were genetically predisposed to writing romances. Along the way to fulfilling her DNA destiny, Delores married an air force top gun who just happens to be of Viking descent. With all those romantic bases covered, she doesn't have to look too far for inspiration.

## Books by Delores Fossen

### HARLEQUIN INTRIGUE

# CAST OF CHARACTERS

*Marshal Slade Becker*—This bad-boy marshal is trying to stop a third newborn from being kidnapped, but Slade has secrets that put him on a collision path with the baby's adoptive mother, Maya.

*Maya Ellison*—A victims' rights advocate who's had her own brush with a violent past, her only goal now is to keep her adopted son safe, even if she has to rely on Slade, a man who could cost her everything.

*Evan Ellison*—Maya's adopted son. He's too young to realize that a vicious kidnapper is after him.

*Randall Martin*—A businessman who hopes the kidnapped babies will lead him to his missing ex.

*Andrea Culbertson*—A nanny for one of the missing babies, but she's also a suspect in the kidnappings.

*Chase Collier*—The flamboyant millionaire who may have adopted a child only so he could use the baby as a pawn in his toxic marriage.

*Nadine Collier*—Chase's trophy wife who never wanted her husband to adopt a child. Did she take the baby to get back at her husband?

*Will Collier*—The missing five-week-old baby who was the first child to be kidnapped.

*Caleb Rand*—The second kidnapped newborn.

## Chapter One

Maya Ellison spotted the man the moment she stepped out of the grocery store.

He would have been darn hard to miss, especially since he was leaning against her car. Except he wasn't just leaning. It was more as if he was lounging while he took in the scenery. Arms folded over his chest. Jeans-clad legs, outstretched and crossed at the ankles.

Waiting.

Maya had no idea who he was. Or what he wanted. But he appeared to be waiting for her.

She walked closer, her steps slow and cautious while she kept her attention nailed to him. Even with the lounging pose, she could tell he was well over six feet tall. Solid build. Dark brown hair that fell slightly long against his neck. Even though he was wearing a black Stetson, the cool October breeze had rifled through what she could see of his hair and had left it rumpled.

He reminded her of an Old West outlaw. And that

was the reason she tightened her grip on the infant carrier that held her son, Evan.

The man lifted his head, snagging her gaze, but he said nothing as he pushed himself away from her car. The simple gesture nearly caused her to turn and run back into the store, but Maya reminded herself she was on Main Street, in broad daylight, no less. Plus, this was Spring Hill, a sleepy Texas town that was as close to crime-free as a town could get.

*Bad things don't happen in Spring Hill.*

It was the reason she'd moved here. A safe haven to raise her child. She hoped she hadn't been wrong about that.

"May I help you?" Maya asked, and silently cursed the polite tone. She added a glare for his leaning on her car.

"I'm Slade Becker," he said, not answering her question. He reached into the pocket of his black jacket and pulled something out. Before Maya could react to the possibility that it might be a gun, he produced a wallet and held it up for her to see.

Not a wallet.

A badge.

She eased a few steps closer so she could get a better look at him and that star shield. It wasn't a cop's badge, but now that she had a better look at him, his steel-blue eyes seemed as if they did indeed belong to a cop. He didn't just look at her. He studied her from the top of her head to her sensible leather walking shoes. Then that gaze went to the carrier.

To Evan.

Because of the way she was holding the carrier and the single plastic bag of groceries, the man could likely only see the top of Evan's head, which was covered by a blue knit cap. Still, even that seemed intrusive, so she turned, hoping that would shift his gaze off Evan and back to her.

It didn't.

Maya decided to do something about that. She gave the carrier another adjustment so that it was as far behind her as she could position it. The shift caused her arm to ache, and she wouldn't be able to stand there long. Not that she intended to do that anyway.

"You're a U.S. marshal," she said, making sure she sounded impatient, which she was. Even though it was a beautiful autumn day, she suddenly wanted nothing more than to get home.

And away from this lawman with the haunting blue eyes.

There was something downright unsettling about him, and it didn't have anything to do with the car-leaning or memorable eye color. Maybe it was his looks. Edgy, along with being drop-dead gorgeous. He was the kind of man she usually avoided but found herself attracted to anyway.

Maya choked back a huff. No way, no how would

she feel anything but wariness when it came to this man. She wasn't at a point in her life where she was looking for a relationship, especially one with a man like this.

"Yeah, I'm a marshal," Slade confirmed, and the wind had another go at his hair. "You didn't know I was coming." It wasn't a question, nor did he wait for her to answer. "I was on my way out to your house, but I spotted your car in the parking lot and stopped."

"But why?"

He opened his mouth, maybe to explain why she would have known he was coming or why he was indeed there, but her phone rang. The sweet lullaby ringtone didn't mesh with the syrupy tension in the air.

Even though she was on an extended leave of absence from her job as a victims' rights advocate, Maya couldn't risk not checking the caller-ID screen to see if this was someone from the office. She set down the carrier and grocery bag and snatched the phone from the diaper bag she had looped over her shoulder. She then picked up Evan again as quickly as she could, making sure she didn't let the stranger get a good look at her baby.

"Saul Warner," she mumbled, reading what had appeared on the screen of her phone. It wasn't a name she recognized.

"That'll be my boss," Slade provided, his rusty

growl of a voice slicing through the lullaby notes. He leaned against her car again to resume his waiting.

Yet another piece to this puzzle. Why would his boss want to speak to her? "Maya Ellison," she answered.

"Marshal Warner," the man greeted. "I'm sorry I'm just now getting around to calling you, but I got tied up with something. It's possible that Slade Becker is already there in Spring Hill."

"He's with me in the parking lot of Hawthorne's Grocery Store on Main Street." Maya met his gaze again. Frowned. "But why is he here?"

Marshal Warner made a slight sound in his throat, as if the answer were obvious. "Because you need someone there with you, and when the FBI put out the request, Slade volunteered."

Okay. "Uh, why would I need a marshal, and why would the FBI request anything that had to do with me?"

No obvious throat sound that time, and Slade's left eyebrow slid up. It was a question. But Maya didn't know what exactly he was asking.

"You've heard about the kidnappings, of course," Warner continued.

Kidnappings? That kicked up her heart rate. She had seen something in the headlines of a newspaper in the grocery store, but she hadn't read the article.

"I haven't heard much news in the past several

days. I just adopted a five-week-old baby, and—"
Maya stopped herself from gushing about the joys
and challenges of being a new mom and remembered she was talking to a federal marshal.

"Who are you?" Maya asked flat out. "Not your
name. I got that. But why are you calling me?"

"The FBI asked us to help and Slade volunteered
his services. Actually, he insisted on personally taking this case. Like the rest of us, he doesn't want
another baby to go missing."

Her chest was suddenly so tight that Maya was
afraid she wouldn't be able to speak, or breathe.
"Why would you think anyone would want to take
my baby? His birth mother willingly gave him up
for adoption. And everything's in order with the paperwork. I should know because I'm an attorney."

The marshal paused. "You really haven't heard?"

"Heard what?" Maya snapped, though her sharp
tone was more from fear than temper.

Another pause, longer than the other. "Marshal
Becker will fill you in." And with that, Warner hung
up.

She would have huffed if her breath hadn't been
stalled in her lungs. "Your boss said you'd tell me
what's going on," Maya relayed, hitting the end-
call button.

He looked around. Another lawman's glance.
"We should sit inside your car while I explain. Best
not to spend any more time out in the open."

The hairs on the back of her neck started to tingle. But Maya didn't budge and she didn't fall back on a polite response grilled into her with her Southern upbringing. "I'm not getting in a car with you. In fact, I think it's time to call the sheriff."

Slade shrugged. "I'm sure Sheriff Monroe already knows what's going on, but he might not have figured it all out yet. The FBI phoned him a little while ago and faxed him my photo, my file and a copy of the police reports on the kidnappings."

"Figured out what?" Her voice was so loud that it woke up Evan, and he stirred in the carrier. Maya wanted to throw her hands in the air but that would have meant putting down Evan again. She wasn't letting go of her baby.

Slade made another glance around. His attention landed and stayed on the car and truck that were stopped at the traffic light just up the block from where they stood. "Two baby boys have been kidnapped in the past couple of days. Both were from the San Antonio area."

Maya swallowed hard. "I'm very sorry for the families." They had to be suffering. She would be completely distraught if she were to lose Evan. Even though she'd only had him a week, she couldn't imagine what her life would be like without him.

"Yeah" was all Slade said.

The one-word response was laced with a ton of emotion, but it was short-lived. His shoulders went back. His chin came up. And anything that he'd been feeling was once again concealed behind that lawman's facade.

"Neither of the babies has been recovered," he continued a moment later. "*Yet.* Now we have to stop any others from being taken."

There it was again. A threat. Not from him, of course. Despite her earlier thoughts of his dangerous and dark air, he probably wasn't a kidnapper. *Probably.* Unless he wasn't really a marshal and this was some kind of ruse to get her to go with him.

Yes, she really did have to speak to the sheriff.

"I have to get home," she insisted. And run by the sheriff's office so she could have a look at this man's file and those police reports.

Maya walked right up to Slade, looked him in the eye and waited for him to back away. He did. Finally. She shoved her phone back into her shoulder bag and used the keypad on the door to unlock the car.

"You're sure you want to go home? Alone?" he added.

Maya huffed and threw open the back door so she could set the carrier in the specially designed car-seat holder. It made strapping in Evan a cinch, which she needed right now because her hands were shaking. Also, thankfully, her son had gone back to sleep. With luck she'd be home before he started to demand his two o'clock bottle. She had some formula with her, but she preferred to feed Evan at home.

Away from Slade Becker.

"I have a security system," Maya let Slade know. "And a gun."

That last part was a lie, plain and simple, but she made a mental note to consider buying one. She tossed the grocery sack on the floor of the backseat and started to close the door so she could then get inside and leave.

"The other families had security systems," Slade informed her.

That did it. Maya had had more than enough. With her hand still on the back door, she whirled around to face the doom-and-gloom marshal. "Look, those kidnappings have obviously concerned you, but I don't live in San Antonio any longer."

"No, but your son was born there." His words were slow and deliberate, as if he was emphasizing each one.

"So? Lots of babies have been born in San Antonio," she pointed out.

He nodded. "About twenty-five thousand each year. Your son was born September 16, a light day for deliveries because on that day only sixty-two babies were born. Twenty-eight were girls, thirty-four were boys. Of those thirty-four boys, twelve weren't Caucasian. So that brings the final figure of possible victims to twenty-two, and two of them are already missing."

"Victims," Maya repeated. The blood rushed to her head. "What are you saying—that someone might want to kidnap my baby?"

"Yeah." He let that hang in the air for several seconds. "Both of the kidnapped babies were Caucasian males born on the same day as your son."

Oh, God.

She heard her own sharp intake of breath but tried to tamp down her reaction. This didn't make any sense. "Why would anyone want to kidnap Evan? Or either of those children who share his birthday?"

Slade took his time shaking his head. "We hoped you'd be able to tell us."

"I have no idea why!"

Again her voice was too loud, and it caused Evan to stir. He whimpered, and his mouth pursed as if he was about to cry. Maya caught onto the car seat and jiggled it gently, rocking him.

"But if you're right, if your numbers really add up, there are twenty babies." She made sure her voice stayed calmer. Hard to do. "*Twenty.* So why would you think someone would come after my child? Why not offer your services to the other nineteen?"

Slade studied a dark green SUV that was slowly making its way past the parking lot. Not a newer-model vehicle but a big sturdy gas-guzzler.

"Because of the sixty-two babies born that day, only four were placed up for adoption," he said. "One girl. Three boys."

Her heart went to her knees. She didn't want Slade to confirm anything else, but she couldn't stop him. Maya could only stand there and try to brace herself for the worst.

The worst came.

"The adopted boys are the ones who've been kidnapped," Slade said, his words echoing through the thick pulse that was now pounding in her ears. "And your son, Evan, is the final one on the list."

## Chapter Two

Because Maya looked ready to fall face-first onto the concrete, Slade took her arm and forced her to sit in the driver's seat of her car. He had no intention of letting her drive off, but he doubted she was capable of doing that right now anyway. Not with her hands shaking and her breath gusting.

"Evan is the final one on the list," she repeated, though her voice didn't have a whole lot of sound.

For that matter, she didn't have much color, either. The natural blush had drained from her cheeks, leaving her bone-white.

She groaned and pressed her fingers to her trembling lips. A helpless, panicked sound shivered deep within her chest. "Oh, God. This can't be happening."

Slade didn't want to comfort her.

Okay, he did.

He was a sucker for a damsel in distress, always had been. He blamed that on his upbringing at the hellhole, also known as the Rocky Creek Children's

Facility. There was forever a boatload of people who needed some kind of protection, and he'd always been good with his fists that way. But he didn't want to soothe Maya's fears. He wanted her to realize just how serious this situation was.

He wanted her to need him.

But he'd settle for her just accepting that she should have his services, because he wasn't going anywhere. This was his case.

In more ways than one.

"Move over a bit," he instructed.

Maya looked up at him and blinked. Her eyes were brown. Not just any ordinary brown. More like a really good single-malt scotch. They were a nice contrast to all that flame-red hair that dangled and coiled around her face.

"Why do you want me to move?" She glanced around the parking lot, her gaze landing on each car before she scanned the trickle of traffic on Main Street.

"That's why. I'd rather not be standing out in a wide-open parking lot if the kidnapper decides today is the day he comes after that little boy in the backseat."

She nodded. But she darn sure didn't move. Her gaze came back to his, and she sat there staring at him. "Why should I trust you?"

Good question, but Slade couldn't tell her the real

answer. He certainly couldn't tell her the real reason he'd insisted on this assignment.

"Because you have to," he settled for saying. "Because I can stop the worst from happening. I've tracked down kidnappers like this before, and I can do it again."

Slade put his hand on her arm and gave her a nudge so she'd get moving, but she still didn't slide over.

Part of him admired her defiance. Lack of trust and skepticism were a big help to staying alive in a dangerous situation. But another part of him hated that she was making this so damn hard. They didn't need to be here where it would be next to impossible for him to protect her and the baby.

"You didn't read about the kidnappings," he said, trying a different angle. One that would be hard to hear, but maybe it would be persuasive. "You didn't know this monster nearly killed one of the adoptive parents who was trying to prevent the baby from being taken."

The fear was instant. It flashed through her eyes, widening them, but she shook her head. The wind and the motion sent her hair swishing against the shoulders of the cream-colored top she was wearing.

Without saying anything, she thrust her hand into the bag still looped on her shoulder. For a moment Slade thought she might pull out the gun she said she owned. If she even had one, she didn't have a permit to carry it.

But no gun.

Maya grabbed her phone and frantically scrolled through the numbers. She jabbed the call button.

"Sheriff Monroe," she said. It wasn't a bluff, either. Slade could hear the man's voice on the other end of the line. "I'm in Hawthorne's parking lot, and I've been approached by someone from the marshals—"

Slade waited to see what the sheriff had said that'd caused her to stop, but while he waited, he glanced at the carrier seat. He couldn't see the baby, because he was facing the rear of the vehicle, so Slade leaned a little to the side.

The newborn was wearing a cap that covered his head, and he was snuggled deep into thick blue blankets that hid his body and chin. His eyes were closed. Sound asleep. And his mouth was pursed as if sucking on a nonexistent bottle.

"I see," Maya said.

Her comment would have drawn Slade's attention back to her eventually, but her touch drew it a whole lot faster. Except it was a little more than just a touch. Maya caught onto the sleeve of his jacket and gave it a sharp yank. Her eyes were narrowed now—and he could see the question in all those shades of brown.

What was he doing looking at her baby?

Slade put a quick stop to the looking. Best to keep focused only on convincing Maya to accept his help. Because she had no idea yet just how much she needed it.

"Yes." She continued with her phone conversation. "He's about six-two. Brown hair. Dark blue eyes." She paused. "Right. No visible scars, but I don't see a tattoo."

"Six-three," Slade corrected under his breath. "And yeah, there's a tattoo, but unless you're planning to strip-search me, it's not visible."

That earned him a top-notch glare.

A moment later Maya pulled in a long breath. "So Slade Becker really is a marshal," she commented to the sheriff. "You're positive? Because his hair seems too long for him to be a lawman."

"I just came off a month-long assignment chasing down fugitives and didn't have time for a haircut," Slade provided, though he wasn't sure she heard him. Maya jammed her finger in her left ear as if she intended to shut out anything he said.

She paused again while she continued to throw glares at him. "All right. No. I don't think it's necessary for you to come here, but you're right about it being a good idea for one of your deputies to drive out to my place and have a look around. Thank you, Sheriff."

The moment she ended the call, Maya studied him, specifically his eyes. "The sheriff confirmed your identity. He knew you were coming to town. He'd already left a message on my answering machine at home and has someone headed to my house now to make sure no one is there."

"Good," Slade mumbled. But he wouldn't trust the locals on this. If and when he got to Maya's house, he'd go through it again himself.

"The sheriff said I could wait here until he's made sure everything is safe at my house," she added. She stared at him a moment longer, huffed and then moved across to the passenger's seat so he could get in behind the wheel.

"Thanks." But Slade was pretty sure his tone didn't sound sincere, especially since he was merely thanking her for learning the truth. Still, he couldn't blame her for wanting to confirm his identity. In addition to that one, maybe she'd be willing to take other precautions.

Lots of them.

"What now?" Maya asked.

"We go to your place so I can have a look at your security system." Slade watched her glare turn to a frown. He did some frowning of his own. He wanted to offer her an alternative like a safe house, but he couldn't press this too hard, too fast. He darn sure couldn't have Maya demanding that he be removed from this assignment. "Or we wait here for the sheriff to call."

She looked ready to jump on that second choice,

but then Maya glanced over the seat at the baby. She reached out and touched Evan's hand. Then his forehead. Probably checking to make sure he wasn't too cool or too warm.

Maya opened her door, and with the driver's side still open, the breeze flowed through the car. The breeze also caught her scent and it drifted Slade's way. Something feminine and musky.

It wasn't the kind of scent that came from a bottle.

"We wait for the sheriff's call," she said. "And before I take you back to my house or anywhere else, I want you to fill me in on this kidnapper. You said the cops don't know why the babies are being taken, but you must have an idea."

"Several of them." None of them would make her breathe easier. "There's the obvious—maybe this person is a baby snatcher. A woman who either is unable to have a child of her own or has recently lost one."

Of course, that didn't explain why she'd take two babies, both of them adopted.

"You have any suspects?" she asked.

"Just a person of interest who's missing, but the FBI, Marshals and the police are going through records and searching for any eyewitnesses."

Slade caught a flash of green out of the corner of his eye and looked in the direction of the traffic light again.

*Hell.*

There was the green SUV again. It'd just come this way several minutes earlier.

"Is something wrong?" Maya asked.

He glanced at her and confirmed she had followed his gaze to the SUV. "You recognize that vehicle?"

"No. But it's fall break for some of the schools. It could be someone visiting from out of town." She sounded hopeful. And concerned.

Slade took out the small notepad and pen from his jacket pocket and jotted down the license number. Maya was probably right. It could be nothing, but with the other kidnappings, he had to assume it could be something.

"Is that how the other babies were taken?" Maya's attention stayed on the green SUV. "Someone grabbed them from a public place and drove away with them?"

Slade nodded. "The second one went down that way. The adoptive mother was coming out of her pediatrician's office in downtown San Antonio. It was late. She had the last appointment of the day, and as she was getting into her car, someone bashed her on the back of her head. When she came to, her baby was gone, and there were no witnesses to the crime."

The traffic light changed, and the green SUV started to inch forward. The windows had a heavy tint, but he could just make out the silhouette of the driver. A man, judging from the size. There didn't appear to be anyone else in the vehicle.

"And the other kidnapping?" There was a lot of breath in her voice, and Maya was watching the SUV as if it were a jungle cat stalking them.

Slade almost hoped it was indeed the threat that his body was preparing to take on.

A showdown.

Right here, right now.

Part of him wanted nothing more than to stop this dirtbag and put an end to the danger. But he also didn't want a shoot-out with the baby in the backseat.

He put Maya's question on hold for a moment, took out his phone and called the dispatcher at the marshals' office in Maverick Springs. All five of his foster brothers worked there. All five would do whatever he needed. But Slade didn't want his brothers to know about this yet. In case it turned out to be nothing.

The agency dispatcher answered right away, and Slade read off the numbers of the license plate.

"Call me when you know who owns the vehicle," Slade instructed. He put his phone back in his pocket and slid his hand over his gun, which was in a waist holster concealed beneath his jacket.

"The SUV isn't stopping," Maya said practically in a whisper.

No, it wasn't. The driver crawled past the grocery

store and headed east on Main. Slade shifted a little in the seat so he could spot the SUV if it doubled back.

Maya's soft gasp, however, had his attention going right to her. "You really think you'll have to use a gun here?" She tipped her head toward his holster.

He thought about answering yes in the hopes of drilling home that it wasn't a good idea for them to be sitting in a parking lot, but she already looked scared enough. "I want to be ready," he said. "Just in case."

"Oh, God." She shook her head and repeated it. "This is for real, isn't it?"

Slade settled for a "Yeah."

Yeah, it was for real, and yeah, all of this was starting to hit her like a sack of bricks.

She pulled off her shoulder bag, dropped it on the floor and folded her arms around her. Her motions were borderline frantic, no doubt matching the intensity of the emotion going on inside her.

"A baby snatcher wants my child," she mumbled.

"Well, that's one possibility." He paused and gathered his thoughts so he could try to word this the right way. "The babies could have been taken to cover up something illegal about the adoptions themselves."

Maya was shaking her head before he even finished. "There was nothing illegal about Evan's adoption. I used a reputable agency and started the paperwork nearly three years ago—"

"You did that after the doctors told you that you'd never be able to carry a child of your own," Slade supplied. But he regretted that little revelation when Maya turned those accusing brown eyes on him again. "I checked into your background. Into all the adoptive parents' backgrounds," he amended. "I was looking for a connection."

"And did you find one?" she snapped.

"No. You're the only single parent of the three. The only one who's an attorney."

Maya huffed. "But there has to be something. Maybe a connection with the parents. Their jobs. Their ages. *Something.*"

Yeah. There was. And that was something she wasn't going to like much. Of course, he hadn't done or said anything so far that would make this a fun experience.

"The parents of the first child own a successful business. Several of them, in fact. The second couple are both teachers. You're thirty-two, and their ages ranged from twenty-six to forty-three. But I don't think any of that information is relevant. I've gone through the files, and the only thing that connects all of you is the fact you adopted baby boys who were born on the same day."

She stayed quiet a moment and stared at the dashboard. "Maybe that *is* the only connection. Maybe the kidnapper is looking for a specific child."

Slade couldn't dismiss that, but there was a problem with that theory. "Neither of the stolen babies was returned."

Still, that didn't mean they wouldn't be or that this particular predator was indeed searching for one child. Maybe a child he'd already found. Maybe not. And maybe returning the babies was just too risky.

Judging from the way she dragged in her breath, Maya had just figured that out.

His phone rang. Not the lullaby tune like the one on Maya's phone. His was the standard annoying ringtone, and after seeing the call was from the dispatcher, Slade knew he had to answer.

"You ran the plates?" he asked.

"I did," Todd Freeman, the dispatcher, confirmed. "The owner's Randall Martin from San Antonio. He owns a bowling alley and has a record for assault eight years ago but nothing recent."

"Ask someone to run a deeper check on him. I want to know if this guy has family or business in Spring Hill. Then check and see if he has a girlfriend or a wife who recently lost a child. It might have even been a miscarriage or fertility problems. I also need to know if he has any connection whatsoever to Maya Ellison or the other two families of the missing babies."

Todd confirmed he would get someone right on that, and Slade ended the call.

"You have a lead?" Maya asked.

He lifted his shoulder. "Just checking all angles."

There was a sound from the backseat. First it was a whimper. But within seconds it changed to a full-fledged cry.

The baby was awake.

"He's hungry," Maya announced. She dug down into the shoulder bag and produced a bottle filled with formula. "I need to feed him."

Slade volleyed glances between their surroundings and Maya while she leaned over the seat. She unhooked the safety belts that held the baby in the carrier and car seat, and she scooped him into her arms.

"Hi, sweetheart," she murmured, kissing the baby's cheek. She returned to a sitting position and cradled Evan in the crook of her arm. He latched on to the bottle the second it touched his mouth.

Despite the horrible news Maya had just learned about Evan possibly being in danger, she smiled at the baby and continued to mutter things to him.

But Slade didn't hear what she said.

That's because his heartbeat suddenly got the best of him, and he couldn't hear over the sudden roar in his ears. He could only sit there, watching. Staring.

And wondering.

Maya pulled off the little blue cap and Slade's

heart pounded even harder. He saw Evan's dark hair. He saw the baby's eyes.

Blue.

All babies had blue eyes, didn't they?

He couldn't let his mind run wild. He darn sure couldn't jump to conclusions.

But that was exactly what he was doing.

Maybe all babies had blue eyes, and plenty had dark hair. However, Slade thought that maybe he could see himself in that tiny face. His features. His blood.

His baby.

God, was this his son?

## Chapter Three

Maya was glad she was holding Evan. Just having him in her arms steadied her and reminded her that she couldn't fall apart. She had to face this danger head-on because she didn't have a choice. She had to do everything within her power to keep her baby safe.

She glanced up from Evan to see the sheriff's white cruiser pull into the parking space next to her car. The tall, lanky lawman stepped out and he tucked a manila folder beneath his arm. Hopefully, he hadn't come there to tell her there was a problem with the security at her house.

And then Maya caught Slade's gaze.

He wasn't looking at Sheriff Monroe. Or even at her. He had his attention fastened to Evan. As he'd done in the parking lot, he examined Evan's face, with his forehead bunched up as if he was trying to figure something out.

"Maya," the sheriff said, approaching her car. He stooped down so he could see inside and looked past

Maya and at Slade. "Marshal Becker. I'm Sheriff Wilbert Monroe."

Slade nodded, acknowledging the introduction, but he was still staring at Evan. And that wasn't alarm he was showing. Too bad Maya couldn't figure out exactly what was behind the marshal's intense expression.

"I checked your house," the sheriff said to her. "No sign of anything out of the ordinary, but none of your neighbors was home. Would have been nice if they'd been able to tell me if there'd been any unusual vehicles in the area."

Maya nodded and gave Evan's bottle an adjustment. "But there might have been a suspicious vehicle near here." She leaned closer to grab Slade's attention so he'd quit looking at Evan.

He did, and for a moment he seemed as if he'd been pulled out of a daydream.

"Marshal Becker's having someone look into it," she explained. "But after we have answers about that, I'd prefer someone else guard Evan and me."

The silence was instant, and Maya glanced at both of them. The sheriff looked a little surprised, but it was Slade's reaction that she noticed most. Was that anger she saw in his eyes? Whatever it was, it was powerful stuff.

"I see," the sheriff finally said. "I'll make some calls—"

"You don't have time to hire anyone else," Slade

interrupted. He turned his attention to Maya. "This kidnapper isn't going to wait for you to put security in place. He'll probably hit today."

Today? God, so soon?

Maya had to tamp down her nerves so she could speak. She also had to loosen her grip on Evan's bottle. The hard plastic felt ready to snap. "I'm sure the sheriff will assign a deputy for protection until I can get a bodyguard out here."

"A deputy." Slade repeated it like profanity, and he turned toward her so they were facing head-on. "Look, I know you have a problem with me. My hair's too long. I don't look like a marshal. Heck, I think you're even scared of me. But I don't want any of that to stop you from getting the best protection for that baby." He rammed his thumb against his chest. "And I'm the best."

"He's right," Sheriff Monroe agreed, apparently taking up his cause. "My deputies have been trained, but according to his file, Marshal Becker has more experience than all of them put together."

Maya didn't doubt that, but she doubted she'd be comfortable with this man. But she immediately rethought that. One of the main reasons for her discomfort was this tug she felt deep within her belly. Slade was attractive, and she was attracted to him. But she was also smart enough to know he was hands-off.

Plus, there was the way Slade had looked at Evan.

That was unsettling, too. It was almost as if this case was personal to him. And maybe it was. Maybe he, too, had lost a child.

Still…

Maya shook her head, but she didn't get to repeat that she wanted another bodyguard, because Slade spoke before she could.

"I'll protect Evan with my life," Slade insisted. "I won't fail at this."

Maya stared at him. And despite all her other concerns, she knew what he was saying was the truth. He would protect her son at all costs.

Later she wanted to know why.

But for now she'd settle for answers that would help her make a decision about whether to keep him as a temporary bodyguard.

"What makes you think the kidnapper will strike today?" Maya asked Slade.

"The first kidnapping happened day before yesterday. The second, twenty-four hours later. At five p.m. another twenty-four hours will have passed."

Maya checked her watch. That was only about three hours from now. Not nearly enough time to find a bodyguard and get him out to her house. Heck, it might not even be enough time for the sheriff to assign her a deputy and have him in place, since that would no doubt involve juggling some schedules.

"The police and FBI don't have anyone in custody," Sheriff Monroe continued. "They're narrowing down suspects, but it could take precious time for them to get close to making an arrest. What we need is for the marshal here to capture this person so the danger will be over and the kidnapper can tell us where the other babies are."

Of course. The families of the missing children would be well past the point of waiting on pins and needles. They'd be in panic mode.

"But Slade has no idea who might come after us," Maya pointed out. "This could turn dangerous, and I don't want Evan used as bait."

"He's already bait." Slade's mumbled words seemed to echo through the car.

Worse, Maya couldn't deny that it was true. The kidnapper might already have Evan in his line of sight.

"According to the info the marshals sent over, they're looking into several possibilities as suspects," the sheriff continued, drawing Maya's attention back to him. "There's a woman, Andrea Culberson. She's a nanny who might have kidnapped her employer's baby. He was the first child taken who shares Evan's birthday."

"Andrea Culberson," Maya repeated. The name meant nothing to her. "They're sure she took the baby?"

"Not sure at all. She's missing, and someone burned the Colliers' estate to the ground. If she's not the kidnapper, then it's possible the real kidnapper did something to make her go on the run. Or maybe just did something to *her*." The sheriff extracted a three-by-five photo from the file and held it out for Maya. "That's Ms. Culberson. Have you seen her before?"

Maya studied the photo of the woman with spiky blond hair. She was young, mid-twenties at most. "No. I don't think so."

"The police don't know where she or the baby is," Slade provided. "She disappeared, and since then her former employers have discovered that she had some problems."

"What kind of problems?" Maya asked, afraid of the answer.

"Depression, for starters. Andrea Culberson had a miscarriage exactly a year prior to the first kidnapping. It's possible she's taking the children to make up for the one she lost."

Extreme measures, but they might not seem so extreme to someone who was desperate for a child. Maya understood that desperation. To a point anyway. She'd wanted a child with all her heart, but she wouldn't have resorted to kidnapping.

Maya studied the photo, committing the woman's image to memory. She prayed she didn't come face-to-face with Andrea Culberson anytime soon.

"Plus, there's another possible suspect," Slade

continued. "The person who's behind the wheel of the green SUV that circled the parking lot."

"Yeah, I got a call from the marshals about that SUV on the drive over," the sheriff added. "We're trying to get a photo of the owner, Randall Martin."

A photo would help. Well, maybe. It would at least alert her if she saw someone who looked like Andrea Culberson or Randall Martin. But there was the frightening possibility that it was neither of them.

Evan stopped sucking the bottle, and when Maya looked down at him, she realized he'd fallen asleep. Not good. He would spit up if she didn't burp him, so she eased the bottle from his mouth and placed him against her chest so she could pat his back. The motions weren't routine yet, but she was far more comfortable with her mothering duties than with what she had to do next.

She had to make a decision about accepting, or declining, the marshal's help.

The sheriff checked his watch. "I need to head back to the office and bring everyone up to speed on what we've learned." He glanced at Slade, then Maya. "I hope you'll allow Marshal Becker to go with you to your house, at least until we can make other arrangements."

Maybe. The verdict was still out on that. Maya

couldn't dismiss the way Slade had looked at her baby. "I'll think about it."

The sheriff gave a frustrated sigh, aimed another glance at Slade that smacked of *Convince her* and walked back toward his car.

Slade shifted in the seat so he was facing her again. "What part didn't you understand when I said it was dangerous for us to sit here in the parking lot?"

"Oh, I understood all the parts. I'm just not sure I can trust you."

She didn't know who was more surprised. Maya, for actually speaking her mind, or Slade, for being on the receiving end of it. Something went through his eyes. Hurt feelings, perhaps? Or maybe it was something deeper than that.

"Did you lose your own child or something?" Normally that was a question she wouldn't ask, either, but this was far from a normal situation. She needed to understand Slade's response to Evan.

Slade didn't look at her. He started surveillance of the parking lot and traffic light again. "Yeah."

So that explained the long look he'd given Evan. Well, maybe. "There's more," Maya insisted.

She waited for him to deny it or to tell her that it was none of her business, but he sat there silently for several moments before he spoke.

"I had a relationship with a woman that ended, well, pretty bad."

There was no good way to respond, so Maya just waited for him to continue.

"Months after things were over between us, I found out she was pregnant with my child." Slade paused, and even though he didn't move even a muscle, she could feel the storm brewing just beneath the surface. "She disappeared before I could find her or the baby."

Maya automatically pulled Evan closer and kissed his cheek. "I'm sorry."

Well, that explained why he'd volunteered for this case. Now, the question was—did she intend to let him help her?

Maya glanced at Evan. Then at Slade. And she knew she had to do everything to protect the precious baby in her arms. Everything, including accepting temporary help from this man.

"All right," Maya said.

That was apparently all the confirmation Slade needed, because he put out his hand. "I'll drive, but I need your keys."

Maya first leaned over the seat and strapped Evan back into his carrier, and then she retrieved the keys from her bag on the floor. She reached out to hand them to Slade, but movement caught her eye.

It caught Slade's, too.

His head whipped toward the back of the parking lot. Maya followed his gaze and saw the green

SUV. The same one that she'd noticed at the traffic light earlier. But it was no longer at the light.

There was a squeal of the tires, and the green SUV came right toward them.

## Chapter Four

"Get down!" Slade shouted to Maya.

He drew his gun and pushed her lower onto the seat. It wasn't a second too soon, because the green SUV slammed into their front bumper, jolting not just Maya's vehicle but the two of them. Evan, too.

The baby immediately started to cry.

Slade had tried to brace himself for something like this, but bracing obviously hadn't done a darn thing to stop it. Here they were right in the middle of what had to be a kidnapping attempt.

Or maybe even something worse.

After all, the kidnapper had already tried to kill one of the adoptive parents, so it wouldn't be much of a stretch to guess that he would attempt murder again.

The green SUV shot past them, the back end clipping Maya's car, but the vehicle didn't speed away as Slade hoped it'd do. With the tires squealing, the driver did a doughnut in the parking lot. He didn't bolt forward, but Slade heard the driver rev up the engine. The revving wasn't nearly as much of a concern as was the SUV's position.

It'd blocked the exit.

"I need the keys," Slade insisted. And despite her hands shaking like crazy, Maya somehow managed to give them to him.

Slade started the engine, kept his gun ready, but that was all he could do. There was no way out unless Slade tried to bash the vehicle from the front of the exit. Not a wise choice since the SUV was bigger than Maya's car.

His other option was to stay put and hope the sheriff would arrive in time to scare this guy off, because Slade wasn't sure he could drive over the foot-high concrete barrier that divided the parking lot from the sidewalk. He'd wreck for sure, maybe even collide with other cars traveling on the street.

And even if they weren't hurt in all of that, it'd make them sitting ducks.

Besides, he needed to be able to aim in case this guy started shooting. With the other customers in the parking lot and the wall of glass at the front of the grocery store, Slade didn't want this bozo firing shots.

The fear crawled down Slade's spine. He'd hoped to have had the baby in a safe place before confronting this kidnapper, but it was too late for that.

The kidnapper was here.

And the stakes were sky-high.

Even if that baby in the backseat wasn't his, Slade couldn't let the newborn be taken. God knows what this SOB had done with the two children he'd already kidnapped.

Maya didn't stay down. Despite the fact that Slade was practically on top of her, she fought to get away.

"Evan," she repeated.

Slade knew that her every instinct was probably screaming for her to get in the backseat with the baby. His certainly were, and while it was a risk for her to move, it was an even bigger risk for him to have to struggle with her when he should be getting them away from the danger.

But the danger came at them again.

The driver jammed his foot on the accelerator just as Maya crawled over the seat. Slade didn't bother to check and make sure she was using her own body to protect Evan. She would be.

"Hold on," he warned her, and Slade threw the car into gear.

He didn't completely manage to avoid a collision with the other vehicle, but he stopped them from taking a direct hit. Still, he heard Maya's sharp gasp of surprise, and he felt her slam against the back of his seat. Thank God the baby was strapped in and semiprotected. But Slade wasn't sure how much longer Maya's car could hold up with this battering.

The green SUV backed up, and just like before,

it came at them again. Slade jerked the steering wheel to the right, but there wasn't enough space for him to get them away from the impact. He grazed a van with what was left of the front bumper, and the driver plowed right into the passenger's side of Maya's car, crushing it in so far that the door ended up near the gearshift. So did the sheet of safety glass that was knocked from the window.

"Stay as low as you can," Slade shouted out to Maya. "And if you can, call 911." Though someone had no doubt already done that. Still, the sheriff needed to know what he'd be up against when he came rushing to the scene. "Tell them the person in the SUV is attacking us."

Evan's screams were louder now, but Slade tried to tune out the sounds and focus on what he had to do.

And what he had to do was stop this idiot.

Yeah, it was a risk, but anything was at this point. With the glass gone from the window, Slade had a direct shot at the SUV.

He took it.

The bullet he fired was deafening, even over Evan's cries and the roar of the engines, and it tore through the front windshield. The safety glass cracked and webbed, but it didn't give way, and that meant Slade didn't even get a glimpse of the driver.

The guy was no doubt armed.

And that's why Slade threw the car into Reverse

and got out of the line of fire. He figured the kidnapper wanted the baby alive and that he wouldn't shoot. Still, Slade wanted to put as much distance as he could between them and the SUV. Backward he flew across the parking lot and tried to dodge as many cars as he could.

"Someone's trying to kidnap my baby," he heard Maya relay to whoever had answered her 911 call. She gave the info about the SUV and the location and then begged the person to hurry.

She sounded many steps beyond frantic, on the verge of all-out panicking. No surprise there. This was probably the first time in her entire white-picket-fence life that she'd been attacked. But Slade hoped she could hold it together. The last thing he needed was her to be hysterical.

Slade finally heard a welcome sound. Sirens. Thank God the sheriff was on the way. Better yet, the kidnapper must have heard it, too, because the driver turned the SUV. Not toward Maya's car…but in the opposite direction.

He was trying to escape.

Hell.

That definitely wasn't good. Slade wanted to stop him. Wanted to drag him from the SUV and beat some answers out of him. There were two missing babies, and this same moron had just tried to take another.

"Wait here," Slade ordered Maya.

He reached to open the door, but reaching was the only thing he managed to do before he caught the movement from the corner of his eye.

Not the SUV.

But there was someone seated in a black two-door sedan parked in the corner of the lot. He'd noticed the vehicle, of course, when he'd first arrived at the grocery store and spotted Maya's car.

But he darn sure hadn't seen anyone inside.

Well, he saw that someone now—the shadowy figure behind the steering wheel—and an uneasy feeling snaked through Slade. He'd been a marshal for nearly ten years, and that was more than enough time for him to sense something was wrong.

Slade kept one eye on the SUV as it sped out of the parking lot, but he turned his weapon toward the sedan.

Mercy.

Was this some kind of trap?

If so, he'd nearly fallen for it because he had been within a split second of running after the SUV. If he'd done that, it was possible that he would have left Maya and the baby completely vulnerable to an attack.

Slade stayed put. Not easy to do. His body was in the fight mode, but he also felt something else. That overpowering instinct to protect this child. He'd never considered himself father material. And maybe he wasn't. But that didn't seem to matter to whatever was firing the emotions inside him. If necessary, he would die to protect the baby.

Slade glanced at the green SUV as it disappeared out of sight. The sirens got closer, and thankfully the cruiser didn't pull into the parking lot. The driver went in pursuit of the SUV. Good. Maybe the locals would manage to collar the guy—alive—so that Slade could question him.

But that left the person in the black car.

Maybe it was just a case of wrong place, wrong time, but Slade wasn't taking any chances.

"What's going on?" Maya asked. She would have no doubt lifted her head to look over the seat if Slade hadn't pushed her back down.

"There might be a second kidnapper."

Her breath rattled in her throat. "What do you need me to do?" The question rushed out with a rise of breath.

"You're doing it. Just stay down." Maya had already plastered herself over the baby again, and thankfully Evan's cries were now just soft whimpers.

Even though the windshield of the black car was heavily tinted, Slade detected some movement inside. The driver started the engine but didn't move. He just sat there as if daring Slade to come and get him. Slade figured if he did that, he'd be instantly gunned down.

The moments crawled by, and though it seemed

to take an eternity, Slade figured it was less than a minute before he heard a second siren. Backup. This cruiser, too, might go in pursuit of the SUV, but if it turned into the parking lot, that would free up Slade to check out his theory about the second kidnapper.

Except the kidnapper obviously had a different plan.

The black car inched forward, and Slade cursed. Because he thought the guy was about to bash into them again. Slade took aim at the driver but held back pulling the trigger just in case this turned out to be nothing.

But it sure didn't feeling like *nothing*.

The driver didn't come toward them but instead turned toward the exit. He didn't screech out as the SUV had done. He simply drove away as if he'd finished whatever routine business he had.

"You recognize that car?" Slade asked, and he made a mental note of the license plate.

Maya lifted her head just a fraction and looked over the seat and Slade's shoulder. "No. But if he's the kidnapper, he's getting away."

Slade was well aware of that. "Call 911 again and give the dispatcher a description of the vehicle. I want this guy followed." Slade rattled off the license plate that he hoped wasn't fake.

Maya made the second call, but this time she didn't stay down when she finished. She watched the black car drive out of the parking lot. Again, not hurried. The driver was doing nothing that would draw attention to himself, but the fact that he'd been there during the kidnapping attempt drew all of Slade's attention.

Two vehicles, two drivers. And it could be just the tip of the iceberg. Maybe the kidnapper wasn't working alone, and if so, it only proved just how determined this guy was.

But why?

If someone was kidnapping babies for emotional reasons, then an attack like this didn't make sense. The person in the SUV had been determined. Desperate, even.

And that brought it all back to Slade.

"What's wrong?" Maya asked. "You're breathing funny."

Slade hadn't noticed any change in his breathing, but he immediately tried to fix it. He didn't want to have to give Maya an explanation that the kidnappings could be connected to him.

But they could be.

Yeah, it had crossed his mind, but it was something he'd tried hard to dismiss. Well, he couldn't dismiss it now. There were some criminals he'd arrested who would no doubt like to give him a dose of revenge. What better way to do it than to kidnap his child and use the baby to get back at him?

Slade mumbled more profanity. He needed answers. About Deidre. About her death. About everything. Because if this was indeed connected to him, he had to stop it.

And learn if one of these three baby boys was his.

In fact, the kidnapper might already have his child. That only made his stomach knot even more, but Slade couldn't dismiss the punch of emotion he'd gotten when he looked at Evan's face. He wasn't the sort of man to believe in woo-woo junk, but he couldn't deny that he'd felt…something.

Something he pushed aside when the police cruiser came flying into the parking lot.

Maya lifted her head again. "It's Sheriff Monroe." And she might have bolted from her vehicle if Slade hadn't caught onto her and held her in place.

Her eyes widened, and she shook her head as if considering the impossible. "You think someone else is out there?" But she didn't wait for his answer. Her gaze fired all around the parking lot.

"We don't know how many people this kidnapper could have hired to help him," he settled for saying.

Slade kept hold of her until Sheriff Monroe and a deputy exited the cruiser. Both lawmen had their weapons drawn, and like Maya, they were looking for any sign of danger.

Unfortunately, the danger had driven away.

Slade stepped from the car but motioned for Maya to stay put. "Please tell me you have someone in pursuit of the SUV and the black car," he said to the sheriff.

Monroe nodded. "I've called for backup and road-blocks."

Slade hoped that would be enough. If they got lucky, the missing babies might even be in one of the vehicles. Though it was an unsettling thought to consider the babies—any babies—going through that kind of danger.

"Did you get a good look at either driver?" Monroe asked.

"No." And Slade knew that would be the first of many questions he'd have to answer the same way. On the surface the attack might have looked sloppy and unplanned, but Slade figured the opposite was true.

The deputy stayed diligent, looking around, and Sheriff Monroe hurried past Slade and made his way over to Maya. "Are you okay? Were either of you hurt?"

Maya shook her head, but she was far from okay. Slade could see the terror and the wildfire adrenaline on her face and in her eyes.

Slade went closer, too, and was relieved when he saw that the baby had not only stopped fussing but had fallen asleep. He wasn't sure how that was possible, but he was grateful for it.

"My truck's over there." Slade tipped his head to the side of the grocery store where he'd parked.

"I can drive you to the sheriff's office, and we can wait there until we figure out the next step."

"Not home," she mumbled.

And it wasn't a question. Yeah, the impact of the danger was really starting to settle in now, but she still managed to give him a look that Slade had no trouble recognizing.

She didn't trust him.

Too bad. He hadn't exaggerated when he'd told her that he was her best shot at keeping the baby safe.

Slade took her by the arm and helped her stand. Good thing he didn't let go, because Maya wobbled and landed with a smack against him. Despite the hell they'd just been through, Slade felt another jolt. Not from the danger this time but from the realization that Maya was a damn attractive woman.

And she was in his arms.

She quickly remedied that. "Sorry." She pushed herself away from him but not before Slade caught another look in her eyes. Not distrust.

Oh, man.

He had to be wrong, but it seemed as if there was that little spark. Well, he had too much on his mind and plate to be dealing with that, and he told his body, and hers, to knock it off.

Maya reached for the baby, wobbled again and Slade stepped around her to unstrap the carrier so he could lift it and the car seat. He didn't have anything resembling a car seat in his truck, and the baby had already been put in enough danger.

Clearly, Maya didn't like him handling her baby even while Evan was in a carrier, but even she couldn't argue that she wasn't steady enough on her feet to make the short trek across the parking lot.

Slade kept his gun ready in his right hand, shifted the carrier to his left and gave Maya a nudge to get her moving. However, they only made it a few steps before the sheriff's phone rang.

"Sheriff Monroe," he answered, and Slade saw the immediate change in the lawman's body language.

That stopped Slade in his tracks. Maya, too. Hell, Slade hoped this wasn't bad news, because they'd already had enough of that today. Him and Maya and waited and fortunately didn't have to wait long.

"We got him," the sheriff announced the second he ended the call.

Maya made a sound of sheer relief. But not Slade. He just waited for the sheriff to continue.

"Well, we got one of them anyway," Monroe explained. "My deputy just cuffed the driver of the black car and he's taking him to the sheriff's office now."

"Is he talking?" Slade immediately asked.

The sheriff shook his head.

Slade got Maya moving again. "I'll do something about that."

One way or another, Slade would get answers. And not just about the kidnappings but about the baby's paternity. The moment he had Maya and the baby inside his truck, he took out his phone and started a text to send to one of his brothers.

"Please tell me nothing else is wrong." Maya leaned over as if trying to see what he'd typed.

But Slade fired off the text before she could see it. At least he thought he had.

Maya looked up at him with suddenly accusing eyes. "Why…?" That was all she managed to say for several seconds. "Why did you ask for a DNA kit?"

## Chapter Five

Maya groaned when she checked the clock on the office wall again and wished the minutes would stop crawling by and speed up. It'd been nearly an hour since Slade and she had arrived at the sheriff's office. Almost immediately he'd disappeared into the interrogation room with the sheriff and their kidnapping suspect.

The man from the black car.

No one had filled her in on what the man's role had been in the kidnapping. Or if there'd even been a role. Basically, she'd just been left in the room with the promise from Slade that he'd get answers. Well, that wait for answers was testing her already frazzled nerves.

She was thankful that her son wasn't in on that frazzled part. She'd given him the rest of his bottle not long after they'd arrived, and the full tummy did the trick because Evan was sound asleep.

Unlike Maya.

She was too exhausted to pace across the sheriff's

private office, but she couldn't stop her mind from racing. The attack in the parking lot was partly to blame for that.

*Mostly to blame.*

But some of that mind racing was because of the cowboy-lawman in jeans and a Stetson who'd rescued Evan and her. She should be thanking him a hundred times over, but it wasn't a boatload of thanks that was in that whirlwind inside her head.

It was the uneasy feeling she had about him.

Since she wasn't about to lie to herself, she admitted part of that uneasiness had to do with his looks. Alarmingly handsome. With a dark and dangerous edge. It wasn't even the *edge* that troubled her. In fact, that only made parts of her body notice him even more. But she couldn't shake the feeling that Slade was as uneasy about her as she was about him.

But why?

And did it have something to do with the DNA test he'd requested in the text? Slade hadn't answered her question when she'd asked him about it. There hadn't been time. They'd been in a rush to get to the sheriff's office and he had said something to her about needing to keep watch. Which he had certainly done. She had, too. But she'd soon demand the answer.

The office door opened, and despite her fatigue, Maya jumped to her feet. Just like that her body went on alert, preparing her for another fight. But it wasn't a kidnapper who came through the door.

It was Slade.

He paused in the doorway, looking first at her before his attention landed on Evan. She'd put the carrier on the sheriff's desk because the chair next to her hadn't been wide enough to hold it.

"Did he confess?" Maya asked.

"To some things." And with that somewhat cryptic statement, Slade closed the door and walked closer. His attention was still on the baby, and he sank into the chair next to her.

"His name is Morgan Gambill, and yeah, he has a police record for various drug offenses. He claims someone paid him to go to the parking lot and sit there. He says he didn't know anything about the green SUV, the attack or the kidnappings."

A frustrated sigh left her mouth. "You believe him?"

He shot her a "What do you think?" look. "I never believe anyone with a record that long, especially a drug user who looks like he'd sell his soul for his next fix."

Maya couldn't help it. She shuddered. This was exactly the kind of person she'd tried to distance herself from. "Who hired him?"

Slade shook his head. "Gambill claims he doesn't know, that it was all done via email and a wire transfer. We'll confiscate his computer and go through the account."

But he didn't sound very hopeful that they'd find anything. And they likely wouldn't. She couldn't imagine the kidnapper making a mistake that would be so easy to trace.

"Gambill wasn't armed when the deputy caught up with him," Slade continued. "But he could have tossed a weapon out the car window. Sheriff Monroe has someone out searching the sides of the road now. How is he?"

Since Slade didn't pause before that last question, it took her a moment to realize he was asking about the baby. "He's fine," Maya practically snapped. "Sorry," she added in a mumble.

Slade's gaze came to hers. Even though she hadn't thought it possible, those blue eyes were even more unsettling when aimed at her rather than the baby.

"How are *you*?" he asked.

Maya considered a lie but figured he'd see right through it. "Scared to death and even more afraid of trusting you."

Slade stayed quiet a moment, that steely gaze still drilling into her, and he nodded. "For the record, I don't trust you much, either. I figure first chance you get, you'll try to ditch me and that'll only put you and that boy in harm's way again."

His instincts were spot-on. She had already considered ditching him.

"I can't do much to change your opinion of me," he went on, his voice a husky drawl with a touch of gravel in it. "Can't deny this attraction between us, either. That won't help," Slade concluded.

Again she considered a lie. Again dismissed it. "Last time I acted on an attraction, I got burned—badly."

"Yeah." For one word, it encompassed a lot.

Sweet heaven. Did he know that she'd been attacked and left for dead four years ago?

No doubt.

Slade was a lawman, after all, and he'd known about her desire to have a child. But it only added another level of uneasiness that he knew about the attack. Had likely seen photos, too. Those nightmarish images flashed through her mind. Always there. *Always.* And she had the physical scars to prove it.

"I learned a lot from that attack," she mumbled.

"Bet you did. It's the hard lessons we remember most."

That was the voice of experience, and she made a mental note to do an internet check on Slade. She was betting he had some secrets.

Dark ones.

"I need you not to run," Slade tossed out there. "This investigation will be dangerous enough without you making it worse."

Maya pulled back her shoulders, about to assure him that she wasn't going to make things more dangerous. But she had to rethink that. What if Slade was her best bet at keeping Evan safe? The marshal certainly seemed determined to do just that. And in that particular area, they were on the same page.

"Let's just get through this," he went on. "And find the person responsible. Find those babies, too, so we can get them back where they belong."

Again, on the same page.

So why did it feel as if she were about to step off a cliff?

"What happens now?" she asked. And Maya hoped she didn't have to clarify that she was talking about the investigation and their current situation. They couldn't stay at the sheriff's office much longer, because she didn't have any additional formula for Evan.

"You'll need to go to a safe house." Slade checked the time. "My brother's working on that. The sheriff will continue to press Gambill and hope he spills something. I don't think Gambill's an innocent as he's claiming, but he's not smart enough to put together something like this."

"What about Randall Martin, the owner of the green SUV?" she asked.

"I talked to him on the phone, and he's coming in for an interview, but he claims someone stole his SUV and that he reported it stolen before the attack."

"You believe him?"

Slade lifted his shoulder. "He knew about the kidnappings. Said he heard about them on the news." He scrubbed his hand over his face. "Maybe he did. But he doesn't have an alibi for the time of the kidnapping attempt. He claims he's been home alone."

So he could be the person responsible and could have reported his vehicle stolen to cover his tracks. "What about the missing nanny, Andrea Culberson? Are the cops still looking for her?"

He nodded. "Looking but with no luck finding her. She's left no money or paper trail."

Maya couldn't dismiss the nanny as a suspect, but there was something about her situation that didn't make sense. "If Andrea took her employers' baby, then why would she take another child and then attempt to kidnap Evan?"

"She had some mental problems," Slade reminded her. "Maybe this is just overkill." He paused. "Or she could be dead. The kidnapper could have murdered her when he took the baby."

Despite the bone-weary fatigue, that sent a spike of panic through her. Maya wanted to get out of there, fast, so that her baby wouldn't be in danger.

As if he knew exactly what she was thinking, Slade cupped his hand around her wrist. Not a rough grip. A barely there touch, something she wouldn't have thought him capable of, not with that strongman's body.

"Breathe," he insisted.

Only then did Maya realize that she'd sucked in her breath and held it. She released it and shook off his grip. But it didn't matter. Just that brief anchor had been enough to help her settle the panic.

"Andrea's employers, Nadine and Chase Collier, have hired a P.I. to look for her," Slade added. "And their baby, of course."

She looked down at her son and couldn't imagine losing him. A parent's worst nightmare. One that Slade had been through himself. No doubt that was the reason for the pain she now saw in his eyes when he stared at Evan.

The sound shot through the room, and because Maya's nerves were right there at the surface, she gasped. It took her a moment to realize someone had knocked on the door. Slade jumped to his feet, moving in front of her, but she saw his shoulders relax when the door opened.

But Maya didn't relax.

The man in the doorway looked just as intense as Slade.

"My brother," Slade said to her. "Marshal Declan O'Malley."

The lanky dark-haired man slipped off his Stetson, caught her gaze and nodded a greeting. Maya noticed not only the lack of resemblance but the different surnames.

"Your brother?" she questioned.

"Foster brother," Marshal O'Malley explained.

Like Slade, he had an easy Texas drawl, but there was a hint of some other accent. His gray-green eyes went from her to Slade and then to Evan.

"The safe house is ready." Declan handed the papers he was holding to Slade. "The background checks you wanted."

Slade took them, and Maya went closer to him so she could see what had captured his complete attention. Randall Martin's name was on the first line. Before she could even scan through the personal info about his address, age, etc., Slade mumbled some profanity.

"Yeah," his brother concurred. "You need to question him."

Maya saw it then. In the paragraph of comments. Randall's girlfriend, Gina Blackwell, had left him several months earlier, and apparently it hadn't been a peaceful split, because she'd filed a restraining order against him.

The restraining order didn't prove that Randall could be involved in the kidnappings, but it was a clue that he could be violent. However, there was nothing to indicate that Randall had believed a baby would help bring his ex back to him. But maybe that was exactly what'd happened.

"Might be best if I take Randall into Maverick Springs for questioning," Declan explained. "This is already federal anyway, since the FBI was called in."

She shook her head. "Does that mean the marshals would handle the case?"

"We already are." Slade's tone wasn't as bossy as usual, but he certainly wasn't asking for permission.

"Before you take Maya to the safe house, you can question Randall at the marshals' office," Declan went on. "And talk to Ranger Morris." He paused, met his brother's gaze. "There's been a…development."

Both men glanced at her, and she didn't think it was her imagination they were considering if they should take this conversation out of the room. But then Slade looked at the baby.

"What development?" he asked Declan.

Even though Slade had obviously just given him the green light to continue, Declan hesitated. Mumbled some profanity. "The Rangers claim they found an eyewitness who puts you near Webb's office at the time of the murder."

Of all the things she'd thought he might say, that wasn't one of them. "You're a suspect in a murder investigation?"

Slade's mouth tightened. "I'm a suspect in a witch hunt," he huffed, putting his hands on his hips. "I was raised at the Rocky Creek Children's Facility."

Oh. Now, that was a place she recognized because it'd been in the news for months. The facility was closed now, but it had a less than stellar reputation. As had the headmaster, Jonah Webb, and about six months ago Webb's body had been found in a shallow grave near Rocky Creek.

But she recalled other facts. Ones that had her shaking her head. "Webb's wife confessed to the murder."

Declan nodded. "But before she went into a coma, she said she had an accomplice."

She turned toward Slade so quickly that she accidentally bumped into Evan's carrier. Startled, her son's hands flew up, and he started to cry. Maya picked him up to try and soothe him, but she needed some reassurance of her own.

"The Rangers believe you helped murder Webb." And it wasn't exactly a question.

Maya hadn't thought it possible, but Slade's jaw tightened even more. "For the record, Webb deserved to spend an eternity in hell, and whoever sent him there should be given a medal. Not jail time."

It wasn't the declaration of innocence she'd been hoping for, but Maya decided to withhold judgment. About that anyway. From what she'd read about Webb, he had been physically abusing the children at the facility he ran. A man who preyed on someone weaker than himself.

Something Maya had some experience with.

And that was the reason she was willing to cut Slade some slack.

She hoped that was the only reason.

Maya was so deep in her own thoughts that she

nearly missed the look that Slade and Declan gave each other. Something passed between them, maybe an entire conversation, and at the end of it, Slade and Declan moved away from her and closer to the door. With their backs to her, Declan whispered something.

"Is this personal?" she thought she heard Declan say. But what she didn't hear was Slade's response. Declan handed Slade something, and when he turned back around to face her, she saw the small plastic bag in his hand.

"It's a DNA test kit." Slade's attention went straight to Evan. So did he. Slade walked back toward her, reached out and touched Evan's cheek.

Evan stopped whimpering and turned his head toward Slade. Her baby studied the dark and brooding man who'd deemed himself their guardian-protector.

"DNA?" Maya shook her head. "You didn't answer my question earlier when I asked about it. You don't think I had something to do with the kidnappings?"

"It's for the baby. For Evan." He paused, kept touching Evan. "You'll need to swab the inside of his mouth so we can see if there's some kind of genetic connection to any of our suspects. Or someone else in the criminal database. It could give us answers as to who the kidnapper is."

Oh.

She took a moment to let that settle in, and it didn't settle in well. A chill went through her, and Maya turned her body so that Slade's fingers were no longer on Evan's cheek.

"We already have the DNA from one of the missing babies—the second one taken. The lab got it from the baby's pacifier. Now we're working on getting samples for the first baby, his parents and from Evan's birth mother and father."

Again Maya had to shake her head. "The birth mother didn't want her identity known. And my adoption attorney said the mother couldn't name the father. She apparently had multiple partners and wasn't even sure who the father was."

"The DNA might tell us that," Declan volunteered. "And if the birth father has a criminal history. It's possible that he heard about the baby and is now trying to find his son."

That chill in her body turned to ice, and because she was afraid her legs might give way, Maya hugged Evan closer to her and sank back down into the chair. As bad as that scenario was, maybe it meant the other babies were safe, that the kidnapper would release them as soon as he learned they weren't his child.

But what would he do with the child that was his?

Maya hugged Evan even tighter.

Declan looked down at some notes he was holding. "I went through hospital records, and Evan's birth mother is Crystal Hanson. We're searching for her so she can give us a sample, but she has a do-not-contact order regarding anything about the baby. We're also hoping that someone who knew her will be able to tell us the identity of the father." He looked up from the notes and at her. "You never met Ms. Hanson?"

"Never. Evan was actually supposed to go to another family, but they had to back out at the last minute. I was the next one on the list at the adoption agency, so two days after he was born, I got the call."

The best call of her life. Of course, now the danger and fear of the unknown were overshadowing her happiness. Maya resented it, too. Yes, it seemed a small complaint in the grand scheme of things, but she wanted to be able to enjoy every precious moment with her son, and this kidnapper was taking that away from her and from Evan.

Slade opened the test kit and handed her the swab. Part of her wanted to refuse the test and bury her head in the sand, but that wouldn't make the danger go away. And besides, this might just be the first step into stopping the danger so they could get on with their lives.

"Just rub it on the sides of his mouth," Slade instructed.

Maya did it as quickly as she could and handed it back to Slade, who put it back into the plastic bag before he gave it to Declan. "I want preliminary results back ASAP."

Declan nodded and opened his mouth to say something. However, the knock at the door stopped him. Again Slade stepped protectively in front of her, and she had to peer around him to see who was in the doorway when Declan opened it.

Sheriff Monroe.

The sheriff looked at Slade. "You know that missing nanny—Andrea Culberson?"

Slade nodded. "Yeah. The one who might be the kidnapper. What about her?"

Sheriff Monroe hitched his thumb in the direction of the dispatch-reception area. "Well, she just walked in."

"She's here?" Maya couldn't believe it. According to Slade, every law enforcement agency in the state was looking for her and even thought that she might be dead.

"She's here," the sheriff verified, then turned to Maya. "And she's asking to see the marshal and you."

# Chapter Six

Slade groaned.

Yeah, he wanted this meeting with Andrea Culberson, especially if she could tell him what the heck was going on with these kidnappings. But he hadn't wanted this to happen until he'd had Maya and the baby tucked away someplace safe. Meeting face-to-face with a suspect didn't qualify in any way as *safe*.

"I'll take Ms. Culberson in the interview room," the sheriff said as he left.

Declan paused a moment, no doubt silently asking Slade if he should hang around. "Get those results to the lab," Slade insisted. "And as soon as you can, I need all you can find out about our visitor, her employers and their missing baby."

His brother didn't question any of that. Declan hurried out. Maya might have hurried out, too, probably so she could confront Andrea, but Slade stepped in front of her and shut the door.

She stopped but not before brushing against him.

Not exactly body-to-body contact, but it was enough for him to feel the heat knife right through him. Heat he darn sure shouldn't be feeling, at least not until he'd settled some things with her.

Like the paternity of the child in her arms.

If that was his son, he would challenge her for custody. And he'd win because he had the law on his side. Best not to allow something stupid like attraction to get in the way of that. Besides, once Maya learned that he was hiding the possible paternity from her, any and all heat between them would vanish in a heartbeat.

"I want to talk to Andrea," Maya said, but then she stepped back, swallowed hard.

"Do you really want Evan in the same room with a possible kidnapper? Because I don't," Slade added before she could answer.

Maya looked ready to start a big-time argument about that, but he saw the fight leave her eyes. "I just want this to be over." Her words were mostly breath, and the weary sigh turned to a slight tremble of her bottom lip. Heck, her eyes even watered.

She'd been strong so far. A real fighter. But this had to be getting to her.

Slade did the exact opposite of what he'd told himself to do. He didn't stay away from her. He slipped his arm around Maya's waist. "Let me question her, and I promise I'll tell you everything she says."

She looked up at him, maybe to see if there was

taken the nanny job after being disinherited by her wealthy folks.

"Marshal Becker?" she asked, her eyes wide. She was also nibbling on her bottom lip.

He nodded. "You asked to see me."

"And the woman whose baby was nearly kidnapped." Andrea's words came out so fast that they practically ran together. "I need you to understand I'm not guilty, that I didn't take Will."

Will, short for William Chase Collier, the adopted baby boy who'd been in her care when both the baby and she had disappeared two days ago.

"Where's Will?" Slade asked, and he didn't bother to sound friendly. In his experience, a badass attitude made things move a lot faster.

"I don't know." Her voice broke, and she caught onto the side of the table as if to steady herself. The tears came. Man, did they. They started streaking down her cheeks, and while they looked genuine, Slade knew that sort of thing could be faked.

"Start from the beginning. Give me your version of what happened, because your employers, Nadine and Chase Collier, insist you kidnapped their child. And for the record, that makes you a suspect in a subsequent kidnapping and another attempt that happened just a short while ago."

She didn't seem surprised about that, only more distressed. Her chest began to pump for air, and

Slade was thankful that she sat down because she looked ready to fall.

"It started two days ago." Her words no longer came out at breakneck pace. She spoke in a ragged whisper. "I put Will down for a nap after his afternoon bottle and then went to grab something to eat from the kitchen. I had the baby monitor with me and was gone a half hour, tops. When I got back, Will wasn't in his crib."

"You didn't hear anyone?" Slade asked.

She shook her head and shoved her hair from her face. "It's a big house. Twenty rooms, and it was also cleaning day. Three maids were coming and going. A crew of handymen, too. None of them saw anything, either."

"There's been no ransom demand," Slade reminded her.

"I know." Her teary gaze came to his. "The kidnapper planned it that way so I'd look guilty." She reached in her pocket, took out her phone and scrolled through the numbers. "He called me just seconds after I realized Will was missing. The number isn't working now. Believe me, I've tried."

The kidnapper had probably used a prepaid cell. Or Andrea could have used one to call herself. Still, if she'd planned this kidnapping, then why was she here? She had to know that she'd be a suspect. Better yet, where was the baby?

"What'd the kidnapper say to you?" And Slade didn't bother to take the skepticism out of his voice.

What little color Andrea had drained from her face. "He said to meet him at the park and to bring money, and if I called the cops, the baby would die." She paused, mumbled a string of *oh, Gods*. "He insisted he had the place bugged, and he'd know if I called anyone."

That wasn't a new ploy. Slade had heard of other kidnappers doing the same. Maybe it was true, maybe not. One of the maids or someone on the work crew could have planted a bug and then even set the fire.

"I told him I didn't have much cash," Andrea went on, "and he said for me to bring him some of Nadine's jewelry. He gave me thirty minutes to get there." She shook her head. "I had to drive like crazy to make it, and I was terrified. I love that baby like he is my own."

Slade got an uneasy feeling of how he would have reacted if it'd been his child being held hostage. Not a good time for that. And he forced his mind back on the interview. "What happened when you arrived at the park?"

"The kidnapper wasn't there, but he called me again." She showed him the second number on her phone. "He said the cops had been alerted that I'd kidnapped Will. I didn't tell them," Andrea insisted.

Slade lifted his shoulder. "If you're innocent, why'd you run?"

"Because the kidnapper threatened to hurt Will again. He said for me to leave, to get far away from the Colliers' estate and that he'd contact me soon. But he hasn't." She pressed her hand to her mouth. "And I heard someone burned the place down right after Will was taken. I couldn't stay in hiding even if I figured I looked guilty. I didn't know what else to do."

Slade caught movement from the corner of his eye and turned to find the sheriff motioning for him to step out of the room.

"Stay put," Slade warned Andrea first, and he went back into the hall, where he would have asked what Sheriff Monroe wanted if he hadn't seen the open door. Not just any door, but the one to the office where he'd left Maya and the baby. And clearly no one was guarding it.

Slade practically pushed the sheriff aside so he could get to the room and see what was going on.

No Maya.

No baby.

"They're in the break room," the sheriff explained, pointing toward the back of the building. He also handed Slade a grocery bag. "It's formula and diapers. I had my wife run to the store and get it."

Slade mumbled a thanks and started to move

again, but the sheriff stopped him. "You should know that Maya's upset," the sheriff said. "She got a phone call that seemed to shake her up, and she said she needed to stretch her legs." Maybe because Slade was cursing a blue streak, Monroe added, "There's no exit off the break room, just some windows."

Windows could easily turn into an exit for someone desperate. He ran, practically knocking into one of the deputies, and he skidded to a stop in front of the door. It took him a moment—a bad, heart-stopping moment—to pick through the furniture and appliances cluttering the room and locate Maya on the sofa. She had Evan in the crook on her arm and a death grip on her phone.

She looked up, her gaze connecting with Slade's, and he immediately saw the tears. Unlike Andrea's tears, these punched him hard in the gut.

"He said he'd kill us," Maya whispered.

That was another punch. "Who said that?" Slade went to her, set down the bag of supplies and looked at her phone when she held it up for him to see the number of the person who'd called fewer than five minutes earlier.

"He didn't tell me his name." Her voice was shaking as much as she was. "Only that if I didn't hand over Evan, he'd kill all of us, including you. He also said he'd kill us if I told the sheriff, that he'd shoot up the place and he'd know if I'd told him."

Hell.

Things were escalating faster than he could keep up. And it was having a bad effect on Maya. Thankfully, not Evan. The baby had fallen back to sleep.

Slade wasn't good at providing a shoulder to lean on, but he figured Maya needed something. He slipped his arm around her and pulled her to him.

It felt better than it should have.

Far better.

"Think hard." He tried to keep his voice level. Hard to do with the emotions and anger firing on all cylinders. "What else did he say?"

"That I was to sneak out of the sheriff's office and meet him at an abandoned gas station at the edge of town. That's when he said he'd kill us all if I didn't come."

He'd probably try to kill them all if they did show up at the gas station. A Catch-22. Whoever was behind this was getting desperate. Or maybe the guy was just stupid. Either way, Maya and Evan weren't getting close to that gas station.

Too bad Slade couldn't, either.

He wanted to meet this SOB face-to-face, but it was too big of a risk to take because this could be some kind of ploy to lure him away from Maya.

But why?

The kidnapper had to know that Slade wouldn't leave them unprotected. But there was the other possibility. A bad one. That maybe the guy had some contact inside the sheriff's office and would indeed know that Maya had told him about the call.

"Come on," Slade said, and he helped her to her feet so he could lead her to the far side of the room, where there were no windows. He also shut the break room door. There was no lock, but at least it would stop someone from walking right in on them.

"What should I do?" Maya asked.

"Nothing. I'll handle this." He moved the car seat and supplies closer to them, too, in case they had to make a quick exit, and he called his brother Harlan at the marshals' office in Maverick Springs.

"Declan just filled me in," Harlan greeted him. "I've been working on those background checks you wanted."

Good. He'd need that information later, after he'd taken some other measures. "Maya got a call from the possible kidnapper." Slade took her phone and read off the number.

Almost immediately, he heard Harlan's fingers clicking on the computer keyboard. "It's a burner," Harlan said several moments later.

"A burner?" Maya asked.

Slade hadn't realized she could hear the conversation, but then, he had her plastered right against him. She was no doubt as desperate for answers as Slade was, and that was the reason he clicked the speaker button.

"A burner is a prepaid cell. Can't be traced,"

Slade explained. Then he added, "Harlan, Maya's listening in now, but the person who called from the burner threatened to kill her if she didn't meet him at an abandoned gas station here in Spring Hill. He wants her to turn over the baby to him."

"I'm not doing that," she insisted, the tears spilling down her cheeks again.

There was the sound of more keyboard clicks. "The name of the gas station is Jasper's. It's been closed for nearly a year now. You want me to get someone out there?"

Slade knew this would alarm her, but he had to say it. "Yeah. But not the locals. Judging from the threat this guy made, he could have a *friend* in the sheriff's office. It's just a precaution," Slade added when her eyes widened, and she stared at him.

"Hold on a sec," Harlan said, and Slade heard him make a call to arrange for some marshals to drive out to Spring Hill.

Those marshals would likely be more of Slade's foster brothers. There were some huge advantages to having five brothers who were all federal marshals, and this was one of them. Slade trusted them with his life.

"Done," Harlan verified. "Now for those background checks." He paused. "You want them now?"

That was Harlan's way of asking if Slade wanted Maya to hear. Slade didn't, not really. She was already too close to falling apart, but Maya's gaze suddenly steeled up.

"I want to hear," she insisted.

Slade mentally debated it but knew whatever he learned from Harlan, he'd eventually have to tell her anyway. "Go ahead," he told his brother.

"You still got Andrea Culberson there in custody?" Harlan asked.

That wasn't the question Slade expected. "Yeah. Why?"

"Because you need to ask her about her employers. She could be innocent in all of this." More keyboard clicks. "I just found out that her boss Nadine Collier is up to her Botoxed forehead in gambling debts. The woman loves betting on the horses, but she's apparently not very good at it. She owes a cool million, and she owes it to the wrong people."

A million. Good grief. That was a big motive for plenty of things. "You think Nadine could have set up the kidnappings to collect the ransoms and pay off her debts?"

"It's possible, especially since her husband, Chase, doesn't seem to know about those debts." Harlan paused again. "The Colliers got a ransom demand about five minutes before you called me."

The demand was actually a relief because until now Slade hadn't known the kidnapper's plans for the missing babies. Maybe this meant the kidnapper wouldn't harm the babies.

Unless…

"Perhaps Nadine didn't kidnap the other baby, only her own adopted son," Slade suggested.

"Yeah." And that's all Harlan said for several moments. "I'm working on it, and if Nadine has her son hidden away, then I'll find him."

Maya shook her head. "So this might have nothing to do with fact that the babies are adopted?"

"We'll piece this together," he settled for saying. Especially since Nadine could still be responsible for all the kidnappings. "How soon can you question Nadine?"

"She's coming in for an interview first thing in the morning."

That wasn't soon enough for Slade. He didn't want Maya to have to go through a night with the danger looming over them. But then, even if Harlan pressed Nadine hard, the woman probably wouldn't confess to kidnapping. She'd no doubt have some well-paid lawyers who would keep her quiet, too.

"Talk to her husband," Slade insisted. "See how he reacts when you tell him about his wife's gambling debts."

"Will do. I'll set up the interview so you can watch it from a laptop. Didn't figure you'd want to bring Maya and the baby here to Maverick Springs to hear the interview in person."

He didn't. It was too big a risk to be on the road with them, and yet he had no choice. Slade had to get her to the safe house. And away from the sheriff's office. Yeah, there was only a slim chance that the kidnapper had an ally here, but a slim chance was still too big of a risk.

"I'll wrap up the interview with Andrea," Slade told his brother. "Better yet, can you send someone out here to finish things with her?"

"Sure. The sheriff does plan to hold her, right?"

"He does. She's a kidnapping suspect."

Of course, if she was the actual kidnapper, she had help since there was no way Andrea could have made that call to Maya. There was also the question of a mole in the sheriff's office and maybe that was the person who'd made the call.

"I know I've loaded you down with stuff, but I have to add one more thing," Slade continued. "Have someone run a check on the sheriff and his whole department. Just in case the caller was telling the truth about that."

"If he was, you shouldn't be there," Harlan insisted.

"I won't be much longer. Call me—"

"Wait," Harlan interrupted. But he was the one who paused. "I need to go over one more thing with you. In private," he added.

Slade groaned. This couldn't be good.

"I want to hear whatever he has to say," Maya insisted.

No doubt. But that didn't mean she should hear it.

Slade clicked the button to take the call off speaker, and he put the phone to his ear.

"What's going on?" Slade asked his brother.

"Declan just dropped off the swab kit with the baby's DNA at the lab, and he said the results are for our eyes only."

"That's right." But he knew what his brother was really asking—why did the results need to stay secret? After all, this baby had been involved in a kidnapping attempt.

"So you want some kind of DNA comparison to prove what—the identity of the birth parents?"

"Yeah."

Another pause. "That's a short answer for a big question. I'll do an entire database search to see if there's a DNA match. But who's the specific DNA comparison we're looking for?" Harlan came right out and asked.

"Mine." He waited for his brother to question that, but Harlan didn't say anything. "Call me when you have the results."

Slade ended the call, shoved his phone back in his pocket so he could carry the car seat and baby supplies but still have his right hand free for his weapon. He prayed he didn't have to pull it, but with everything going on, Slade wasn't going to trust anyone who wasn't family.

"We're leaving," Slade told her. "We'll go out the

side exit, and once we're outside, move as fast as you can to my truck."

She nodded but didn't budge. Maya looked up at him. "I heard," she said in a whisper.

"Heard what?"

Maya swallowed hard. "I heard," she repeated. "Why do you want Evan's DNA compared to yours?"

Oh, hell.

Slade should have remembered that she'd heard the earlier comment made in a phone conversation. The woman had excellent hearing.

And bad timing.

This wasn't something he wanted to take the time to explain. "We'll talk about it later."

Maya caught onto his arm when he opened the door. "No. We'll talk about it now."

He didn't like that determined look in her eyes, but it faded just a bit when they heard the movement. Sheriff Monroe was making a beeline toward them, and he was moving darn fast.

"We have to get out of the building now!" the sheriff insisted. "Someone just called in a bomb threat."

## Chapter Seven

The bad news just kept coming, and Maya was afraid it would even get worse. Judging from Slade's body language and his sharp replies to the person on the other end of his phone conversation, he felt the same way.

Slade had taken or made multiple calls every second since they'd evacuated the sheriff's office in a mad rush. The ride was equally mad, but that hadn't stopped Slade from keeping watch of their surroundings as they'd first gone to the marshals' office in Maverick Springs so he could get a "clean" vehicle. A truck that couldn't be traced back to him or the Marshals. One that he was now driving down the rural road.

Maya had kept watch, too, because she knew this could all be some kind of ploy to get them out in the open so that the kidnapper could try to take Evan.

"I want him found," Slade snapped, and he jabbed the end-call button as if it were the cause of their problems. "They didn't find a bomb, but during the evacuation, Morgan Gambill disappeared."

Mercy. No wonder Slade had jabbed the phone button so hard. "How the heck could that have happened?"

Slade shook his head and looked on the verge of cursing, but he glanced down at the car seat they'd strapped in between them. Evan was wide-awake and appeared to be hanging on every word.

"The deputy said he just lost sight of him," Slade settled for saying.

Great. Now one of their suspects was on the loose. Even if Gambill wasn't the kidnapper, it was entirely possible he was working for the very person who'd tried to take Evan. "Please tell me they managed to hang on to Andrea."

"They did, and my brother Dallas is personally transporting her to the Maverick Springs marshals' office. I'll question her again tomorrow. Along with Nadine and Chase Collier." His gaze met hers. "That means you'll need to stay at the safe house with one of my brothers."

There was a lot he left unsaid in that last part. Slade seemed to be waiting for her to object. And maybe she would.

Slade was keeping something from her, and she wanted to know what. But first things first. Since he'd been on the phone during their entire hour-long drive, she hadn't had a chance to ask some much-needed questions.

"What about the meeting at the abandoned gas station?" she asked. "Did anyone show?"

"No one. That could mean the guy had us under surveillance and wanted to see what we'd do."

She waited but he didn't add anything. "There seems to be an *or* at the end of that."

Slade lifted his shoulder. "He could just be crazy. Or maybe he wants to torment us as much as he can."

Maya had to groan. Neither of those were *ors* she wanted to consider. "How safe is this safe house where you're taking us?"

"As safe as my brother could make it."

For him, that probably meant it was *safe,* but again, she would decide once they were there. "How much longer before we get there, because I'll have to feed and change Evan soon?" Besides, it was getting dark, and she didn't want to be on the roads if she couldn't see if someone was following them.

Slade checked his GPS. "We're only about two miles away."

Good. But there was a downside to that—it wasn't nearly enough time to press him on the part of the conversation that she'd overheard with his brother Harlan.

"My brother learned more about the Colliers," Slade continued before she could say anything.

"First of all, the ransom demand didn't pan out. They claim the kidnapper told them that he'd be calling them back, and it hasn't happened."

Maybe the kidnapper would call, though. And soon. "Did your brother learn anything else about the Colliers?"

"Some. Nothing good, though. According to an acquaintance, their marriage has been rocky for a while, and it was Chase who pressed for the adoption because he thought it would make things better."

She thought about that, shook her head. "How could any agency let them adopt under those circumstances?"

"It was a private adoption, and a lot of money changed hands. This acquaintance also said that Nadine wasn't happy about any aspect of the adoption, that she didn't want to be a parent and resented Chase for dumping the baby on her."

Maya actually shivered and silently cursed the fact that money had put that innocent baby in what seemed to be a toxic home. When the children were found—and she had to hold out hope that they would be—maybe someone would rescind the petition for adoption.

Slade took a turn off the rural road, and she spotted the one-story house just ahead. Other than a barn, there was nothing nearby, and the pastures stretched out on both sides.

"The town is a good ten miles away," Slade explained, "and the locals believe the owner is a city businessman who lends the place out to clients."

That would provide good cover as to why people would be coming and going, but it looked like an ordinary Craftsman-style house, not a fortress.

Slade didn't stop in front of the house. He drove to the back, parked directly next to the porch and began to unhook the car seat at the same time Maya reached for it. Their hands touched.

Gazes met, too.

She hated the warmth that pooled in her body. Obviously, her past hadn't taught her anything, and she pulled back her hand so she could touch one of the scars on her stomach. Her clothes concealed them, but she could always see them in her mind. And it was the reminder of the scars that gave her the attitude adjustment she needed.

"Once we're inside, I'll want an explanation about the DNA," she said.

He didn't dodge her gaze. In fact, Slade didn't have any reaction other than the barely audible sigh that left his mouth. He lifted the car seat, Maya grabbed her diaper bag and the plastic bag with diapers and formula that the sheriff had given them, and they hurried out of the truck. Slade also didn't waste any time using the electronic keypad to open the door.

The moment they stepped into the house, the security system started to beep.

"Is that you, Slade?" someone asked.

The sound of the man's voice caused Maya to gasp, and it took her one breath-stopping moment to realize the person wasn't inside the house but rather had spoken through the speaker mounted on the wall next to the keypad.

"It's me," Slade verified.

The buzzing stopped, and she saw the keypad lights go from red to green. "The security system is armed," the man said. "If you need anything, just hit the panic button. There's one on the wall in every room next to the light switches."

"Will do. What other measures have been taken?"

"There's perimeter security. If someone turns onto the road that leads to the house, it'll trigger the sensor and that'll give you at least ten minutes' notice that someone's coming."

"What if someone tries to reach this place on foot?" Slade asked.

"No sensors for that. We tried it, but the deer kept tripping it. But the windows are bullet resistant. And in case you have to get out in a hurry, the road curves around, so you could leave out back if you had to."

Maya prayed it wouldn't come to that.

"Call if you need anything," the man added.

Slade assured him that he would, and he pressed

another button on the keypad before he walked across the hardwood floor and set the baby on the coffee table in the modestly furnished living room.

*Modest* described what she could see of the rest of the place, too. There was a dining room directly across from them and the kitchen behind them. She figured the three doors on the right led to the bedrooms. Well, hopefully there were at least two because she had no intentions of sharing a bed with Slade.

Without asking her permission, Slade undid the safety belts and took Evan into his arms. Her son didn't fuss. In fact, he stared at the stranger holding him. And Evan smiled.

Yes, smiled!

Maya figured it had to be gas. From all the books she'd read, Evan was still too young for a real smile, but she felt the tightening in her chest. Not jealousy that someone other than her had been on the receiving end of a smile. No. This was something much stronger than jealousy.

It was fear.

"I want answers," Maya managed to say, though she wasn't sure how. In addition to the tightening in her chest, every part of her seemed frozen in place.

He didn't jump to say anything. In fact, he took his time, and he kept his attention pinned to Evan. No smile for Slade, just the raw intensity that had stirred the muscles in his jaw.

"Remember when I told you about my ex-girlfriend?" he finally asked.

Maya nodded. "The one who was pregnant and disappeared."

"Yeah." And that was all he said for several moments. "Well, it wasn't a relationship, more like a one-night stand, but months afterward she called to tell me she was pregnant with my baby. She said she was within days of her due date, and she wanted me to meet her. She was scared and said someone was trying to kill her."

Evan cooed, the sweet sound drifting through the room, and despite the pained look in his eyes, the corner of Slade's mouth lifted. Not exactly a smile, but she thought maybe that was the nearest he came to that particular expression.

"I wasn't sure it was a real threat," Slade continued, "but I drove to her place in Austin only to find it ransacked. And she was missing."

Oh, mercy. Maya didn't like the sound of this at all. "What happened?"

Slade lifted his shoulder, but there was nothing casual about the reaction. There was a storm raging just beneath the surface. "Deidre's body was found a few hours later."

Maya put her hand on her chest to steady her heart. It was racing now, and she wasn't sure she wanted to hear the answer to her next question. Still, she had to know. "And the baby?"

"Missing. He wasn't with her body."

Her heart pounded even harder. "*He?* She had a son?"

Slade nodded. "I managed to learn that from the doctor who delivered the baby. Deidre had paid him to keep the delivery secret."

"From you?"

"Maybe." Another pause. "But she was in trouble, had gotten involved with the wrong man—a guy named Damien Waters—who was jealous that she was carrying another man's child." He mumbled something that she didn't catch. "Deidre had this thing for bad boys."

Something Maya could understand. She, too, had once been there, done that. And yes, she had the scars to prove it.

"From what I've been able to piece together, Waters was verbally abusive. Maybe physically, too," Slade added like profanity. "He's dead now, so I can't get answers from him."

Maya wanted to ask if Slade had been the one to kill this abusive man, but again, it wasn't an answer she wanted to hear.

She waited, breath held, but she had the sickening feeling that she knew where this was going. "This happened a long time ago?"

Now Slade's gaze came to hers. "September 16 of this year."

Evan's birthday.

And the birthdays of the missing babies.

Her heart slammed against her chest. Her breath stalled, only to start gusting in and out. And because she had no choice, she sank down onto the sofa. Everything hit her at once. The realization. The tornado of emotions.

And, yes, the fear.

"You think Evan is your son." Maya didn't wait for him to confirm it. She would have grabbed Evan right out of his hands, but Slade moved, turning his body so she couldn't do that.

"No need for that." Slade's voice sounded like a warning, and she thought for a moment he might use physical force to take Evan.

But he didn't.

He calmly shifted Evan back toward her and eased him into her arms.

"Oh, God," she mumbled, and she just kept repeating it. Maya was aware that she sounded crazy, but considering the circumstances, she had a right to snap. "I thought that happened a long time ago."

"No." His gaze came back to hers. "Put yourself in my place. The doctor who delivered my son confirmed that he was born on September 16, and three baby boys born that same day were put up for adoption. If Evan's not mine, then it means my child is likely one of the other two, and he's already been taken."

*Or worse.*

Slade didn't say the words aloud, but she heard it in his voice. Saw it in his face.

She swallowed hard so she could speak. "Evan's birth mother wasn't named Deidre. It was Crystal Hanson."

"Deidre gave the doctor a fake name, too. Besides, if Waters killed her, took the baby and put him up for adoption, he wouldn't have used her real name."

Maya jumped right on that. "But there was a birth certificate for Evan, and the mother was barely twenty. Deidre was older than that, right?"

"Yeah. But Waters could have faked the name, the age, everything. He was into all sorts of illegal things, including a few forgeries. If he didn't do the paperwork himself, I'm sure he knew where to find someone to do it for him."

She wasn't giving up. Maya wasn't ready to buy any of this, because if she did, that changed *everything*. "How can you be sure Deidre was even carrying your child? From the sound of it, she wasn't a very reliable woman."

"She wasn't," he readily admitted. "But the timing is right for her to have conceived my baby. And she wouldn't have voluntarily given him up for adoption. Deidre could be flighty, but the one thing she wanted most was to have a baby." His jaw muscles stirred again. "In fact, she could have gotten pregnant on purpose."

"And not told you?" she snapped.

He gave her a flat look. "Deidre and I had sex. Nothing more on her part or mine. We weren't in love, not by a long shot. I figure the only reason she called me to tell me about the pregnancy was because she knew she was in danger and that I'd protect her."

Maya wanted to scream for him to stop. She didn't want all these pieces lining up like this. Especially when the pieces kept pointing to a conclusion that couldn't be reached.

"I'm sorry. But you can't have Evan. He's my son." And she hugged him close to her.

Slade didn't challenge that. In fact, for several snail-crawling moments he just sat there. "There'll be toiletries in the bathroom. Extra clothes in the bedroom closets. Oh, and the fridge will be stocked. You should eat, feed Evan, change him and then try to get some rest. You need any help?"

She shook her head so fast that her neck popped. Maya didn't want him touching Evan. And as for eating, that wouldn't happen. Her stomach was churning, but thankfully she had enough formula for Evan. Also, thankfully, her baby seemed to be totally unaware of the nightmare going on around him.

Slade got up and first opened the doors off the

living room. She'd been right about them being bed-rooms. Well, two were. The center one was a bath-room.

"I'll take the bedroom at the front of the house," Slade said, and walked into the kitchen.

Maya tried to level her breathing. Tried to think. But most of all she forced herself not to run. Slade had the truck keys—she'd seen him slip them into his jeans pocket—so she literally had no way out of here except on foot.

But she did have a phone.

She hurried to the diaper bag to get it but then froze when she looked at the phone screen. Who could she call?

Sheriff Monroe, maybe.

Then she remembered Slade saying something about the kidnapper perhaps having a *friend* in the sheriff's office. She didn't want to do anything to lead the kidnapper right to Evan.

Frantically, she scrolled through the numbers she had stored. Her parents had been killed in a car acci-dent when she was in high school. She had no fam-ily except for distant cousins who she rarely saw, but she had friends and coworkers.

And one by one she excluded them.

Anyone she called would automatically be put in danger. And besides, she didn't personally know anyone with the physical skills to help protect Evan.

Sweet heaven, what was she going to do?

Maya caught the movement from the corner of her eye and whirled around. Slade was in the doorway of the kitchen, his shoulder propped against the jamb, and he was eating a sandwich. He was also watching her. Or rather watching her hold Evan while she panicked. But Slade wasn't panicking. He looked much as he had when she'd first seen him lounging against her car.

Well, the same except for his eyes.

Those deep blue eyes were still intense. As was the rest of him. But there was something else there, too. Something she couldn't quite put her finger on.

Wait, she could.

It was the kind of look a father might give a child he loved with all his heart. And that broke Maya's own heart. Because his love might be warranted if Evan was his son.

Slade pushed himself away from the jamb and walked closer. "Keep away from the windows," he said. Not one of his growled warnings that she'd become accustomed to. There was a gentleness in his voice.

He reached in the back waist of his jeans and took out a gun. For one terrifying moment she thought he might aim it at her and demand that she hand over Evan.

But he put it on the coffee table.

"There's no safety on this weapon," he said, "and if you call anyone, don't use your cell. It can be traced. Besides, service out here sucks anyway. Use the landline in the kitchen instead."

Maya shook her head. Was he giving her permission to call someone else for help?

He took out the truck keys from his pocket. They jangled when he dropped them on the table next to the gun. "I'm asking you to trust me, but I won't force you to stay under my protection against your will. Just be smart about it and make sure anyone you involve in this will put Evan's safety first."

It was an out. A surprising one. "You care whether I trust you or not?" she asked.

"Yeah." He didn't sound very happy about that. "Let me know what you decide to do."

And with that, Slade walked away from her and disappeared into the bedroom.

*Chapter Eight*

Slade sat on the bed and watched the line of light seep through the edges of the blinds. It was both a welcome sight and not so much of one.

Yeah, they'd survived the night without someone coming after them, but that sun was rising on what no doubt would be a hell of a day.

There'd been a steady flow of emails and text messages throughout the night. Some were updates on the case. Others were details for the security arrangements for the interrogation of their suspects—Andrea and Chase and Nadine Collier. Slade hadn't considered Chase an actual suspect, but then Declan had added a strange note to the arrangements: "Wait until you get a load of this guy."

Clearly, his brother had seen a red flag or two in the man's demeanor, and that was good enough for Chase to land on Slade's suspect list. But that list, and the interrogations, were just the tip of the iceberg.

Morgan Gambill, the guy who'd escaped during the bomb scare, was still missing. Definitely not good. Because his escape alone was enough to prove guilt of something.

But what?

Slade needed to find out.

Then there was the added annoyance of Randall Martin, the owner of that green SUV, who still hadn't been brought in for questioning. Randall had stonewalled pretty much every agency involved and, fed up, Slade had ordered the man arrested. And it would happen, as soon as he was located. Yeah, Randall had indeed filed a stolen-vehicle report hours before the kidnapping attempt, but Slade was tired of having no answers. Because no answers meant Evan was in danger.

That thought snaked through his head just as he heard the movement. He'd been expecting it but didn't reach for the gun he had on the nightstand beside him. The footsteps belonged to Maya. He'd gotten very familiar with their sound because he'd listened for them during the entire night.

And there'd been a lot of them to hear.

When she'd taken Evan in the bathroom so she could bathe him and then take a shower herself. When she had gotten something to eat from the fridge. And when she had fixed Evan a bottle in the middle of the night and then another just a half hour earlier.

Plenty of opportunities to hear footsteps.

And an equal number of opportunities to worry that he'd made an idiot of a mistake by leaving her those keys and that gun. It'd been a gamble. But it had obviously paid off. The proof of that was when Maya stepped into the open doorway of his bedroom.

She'd changed her clothes. A loose green skirt and sweater top. Nondescript clothes provided by the U.S. Marshals Service, but on Maya no clothes were nondescript. The woman managed to make even baggy attractive.

Something he cursed himself for noticing.

"How's Evan?" he asked.

"Fine. He just finished his bottle and will probably sleep for an hour or two." She stretched out her arms, caught onto the doorframe with both hands. "You knew I wouldn't leave even if I could come up with my own safe house and bodyguard. You knew I wouldn't risk taking Evan away from you. Away from the security you've already put in place."

It sounded exactly like what it was—an accusation. He moved the laptop to the bed and eased his legs off the side. He didn't get up, because he didn't want to give Maya any reason to back out of that doorway. This conversation was necessary, though it wouldn't be pleasant.

Slade lifted his shoulder. "You love Evan, and I figured you'd do whatever it took to keep him safe."

Her mouth tightened, and she looked ready to curse him out. "I wanted to leave."

"Yeah," Slade settled for saying.

The silence came. Man, did it, and it was even more uncomfortable than the stare she was giving him.

"There was a laptop in the bedroom, and I did an internet search on you," she finally said. And that sounded like an accusation, too.

"I bet there was nothing in that search about me being in reform school when I was fourteen. I was pretty much a renegade in those days. Still am."

She flinched. But maybe not from surprise. "No. But there was a lot of info about you and your five foster brothers being raised at the Rocky Creek Children's Facility."

Slade couldn't help it. The name of the place always made him scowl. It was too pretty of a name for a hellhole.

"Your foster father, Kirby Granger, was a marshal, and he got custody of all six of you."

He nodded. "Kirby saved us."

And now someone had to save Kirby. His foster father was going through cancer treatments, and it wasn't clear if the treatments or the cancer would kill him. But added to that, Kirby was suspected of murdering the Rocky Creek headmaster, Jonah Webb.

Yet another name that always caused Slade to scowl.

So did the fact that Kirby wasn't the only suspect. Slade and all his brothers were, too. "I cleared up the question the Ranger had about where I was that night," Slade volunteered. "I was with someone." Angelica Sanchez. Angel for short. And she wasn't nearly as spiritual as her name implied.

"*She* was able to give you an alibi?"

Even though he hadn't said he'd been with a girl, Maya had obviously guessed. Slade nodded. "There's still a window of opportunity where I was unaccounted for, but she managed to make that window very narrow by corroborating the time we were together."

He paused. "Are you going to ask me if I killed Jonah Webb?" Slade tossed out there.

She opened her mouth, closed it and shook her head. "From everything I read about him, Webb deserved to die. I don't have any warm fuzzy feelings for a brute of a man who would abuse children under his care."

No surprise there, but Slade hadn't expected her to cut him even an inch of slack.

He tipped his head to the laptop on his bed. "I did a search on you, too." But he hadn't used just the internet. He'd also gotten a thorough background using some law enforcement contacts.

Even in the dim light, he saw the color blanch from her face. "Like Deidre, I had a thing for bad boys."

He shook his head. "Dominic Luker wasn't a bad boy."

Slade hadn't thought it possible, but she lost even more color with the mention of her attacker/ ex-lover's name. He heard the shivery sound her breath made.

"He was a sociopath," Slade clarified, and decided to end it with that dime-store diagnosis. He seriously doubted that Maya wanted to discuss the details of the attack that had nearly left her dead.

And unable to have children.

Several of the sixteen knife wounds Luker had given her had seen to that. But she hadn't given up. She'd recovered, finished law school and started a nonprofit victims' rights group.

Except recovery maybe wasn't the right word.

Yes, Luker was out of her life permanently since he'd been killed in a prison shank fight. Ironic for a man who loved knifing women.

But Luker had left his mark on Maya.

She had no close friends. Hadn't been in a real relationship since the attack and had basically thrown herself into work. Well, until she'd adopted Evan. According to her coworkers, she had no immediate plans to return to work but would instead live off the modest inheritance her late grandmother had left Maya when she was a toddler.

"So we know each other's secrets," she concluded. She walked closer. Slow, tentative steps. But that wasn't a tentative look on her face. "On paper I suspect neither of us looks like a parent-of-the-year candidate. But given the chance, I'll be a good mother."

Her voice cracked, and there was just enough light now for him to see the shine in her eyes. From tears that were threatening to spill.

There it was again. That punch. And this time, it wasn't from heat between them but from that need deep inside him to comfort a damsel. Not that she was exactly the damsel type, but he'd just brought up some of the worst memories of her life and his sheer presence was a reminder that she might lose her son.

Slade went to her, but when he reached for her, she batted his hands away. "Don't. If you touch me, I'll fall apart."

He had his own reasons why he shouldn't touch, but Slade touched her anyway. He pulled Maya into his arms and braced himself for the tears.

But she didn't break into a sob.

Nor did she move.

She stood there, seemingly frozen in place with her arms down by her side while he held her. It took him a couple of seconds for the *oh, hell* to dance through his head. For her, being held by a man might bring back the memories of her attack, and Slade would have jerked away from her.

If she hadn't lifted her hands.

First one, then the other. And she put them on his waist. Definitely not pushing him away.

Just the opposite.

She inched closer to him until they were body-to-body.

"I hate the danger," she said. "It's broken down a barrier that I've spent years putting up."

He knew all about barriers. Knew that sometimes, like now, they were a good thing. But danger, especially shared danger, could indeed bring down walls and forge bonds that could get them in all sorts of trouble.

And maybe even save them.

The best way to keep Evan safe was for them to work together.

"This has nothing to do with Evan." Her voice was a breathy whisper, so soft. Like the rest of her body. And that scent of hers that dulled his mind just enough that it took a second or two for that to sink in.

"I never thought it did."

"I don't want you to think I'm trying to get close to you," she clarified.

But no clarification was needed. That wasn't the

grip of a woman planning to seduce a man to get him to back off. Or even to soften him up. Her touch was tentative, but the tentativeness didn't make it to her eyes.

Her grip tightened slightly. She inched even closer. "And this has nothing to do with you being a bad boy."

"Good thing. Because I lost my bad-boy status years ago." Yeah, it was a poor attempt to lighten things up, but since she looked ready to shatter into a thousand little pieces, he thought she could use the levity.

It worked.

The corner of her mouth lifted just a fraction. "I don't think it's a status you can lose. It comes with the looks and the attitude."

Her gaze combed over his face. Lingered on the dark stubble that was there. Before her attention went lower, to his chest. Only then did he remember his shirt was wide open.

Oh, man.

He was in trouble here. Yeah, she might not be trying to seduce him, but she was doing it anyway. And for multiple reasons he wanted to keep his hands off her. After all, they might end up in a custody battle.

Or together on the receiving end of another attack.

But that didn't stop him.

Hell, maybe she was right. Once bad, always bad. That was the only explanation Slade could come up with as to why he lowered his head and brushed his mouth over hers.

Maya made a sound of startled surprise. Now she'd pull back. Maybe even slap him into the next county.

She didn't do that, either.

She stared at him as if trying to decide what to do, and while she was deciding, Slade took a nosedive off a cliff. He snapped her to him and kissed her the way his body was begging for him to kiss her.

The taste of her slammed right through him, and it evaporated what little common sense he had left. But it wasn't the taste that made things escalate. It was that little sound she made. A little catch in her throat. The sound not of surprise or protest.

But of pleasure.

She slid her arms around his waist and upped the already bad situation when her breasts landed against his chest. Yeah, she had on that skirt and top, but since his chest was bare and also since she seemed to be wearing the thinnest bra ever, he could feel parts of her that he shouldn't have been feeling.

That didn't stop him from feeling anyway.

It'd been a while since the slow burn had turned into an ache. He generally liked to dive right into sex so he could, well, find relief and then leave. Of course, the leaving didn't happen right away, and despite his badass reputation, he didn't fall into bed with many women.

But there'd be no leaving with Maya.

Nope. He had to stay with her until the danger was finished. Until they had the results of the DNA test.

And maybe even after that, if Evan was his son.

That finally sank into his hard head—his quickly hardening body, too—and Slade moved away from her.

"I don't do things like this," she mumbled, and she made his body beg when she flicked her tongue over her bottom lip.

"Ditto."

She gave him a flat stare that was somewhat diminished because she was flushed with arousal.

*"Ditto,"* he repeated.

"Not with those looks," she added, also in a mumble.

He took her by the arm and put her in front of the mirror. "Look at yourself. You're a knockout."

Maya laughed, but it wasn't from humor. She pulled up her sweater top, and the first thing that caught his attention was her barely there bra and her breasts that seemed ready to spill right out of it.

But then he saw the scars.

They were thin white lines, barely visible in the thready morning light. But he figured this was a case of more than skin-deep. Those scars had cut her to the core.

There was nothing he could say or do to lessen the pain she'd always feel, but Slade wished Luker were alive so he could hurt him for what he'd done to Maya.

Slade reached out and ran his index finger over one of the scars. He barely touched Maya, but she shivered. Not from heat this time.

"It's not exactly a *ditto,* but since you've shown me yours, I'll show you mine." He pushed back the side of his shirt, unzipped his jeans and lowered them and his boxers.

Maya's eyes widened. "What are you doing?"

"Not *that,*" he assured her. Though with the taste of her still in his mouth, getting naked with her held plenty of appeal. Thankfully, he did have some shred of common sense and control left.

*Some.*

"My scar." He stopped lowering his clothes at about the midhip-bone point so she could see the healed wound.

She leaned down for a closer look. "You were shot?"

"Yep. By a meth-head federal fugitive I was try-ing to arrest. She said she was aiming for my…fam-ily jewels," Slade settled for saying.

"She nearly succeeded." Maya reached out as if to touch the scar but jerked back her hand. No doubt

because she realized it was indeed just inches away from a still-very-aroused part of him.

"My injury was paltry compared to yours," he went on, "and it didn't come at the hands of someone I thought I could trust. I just wanted you to see that scars are just that. Scars. They don't lessen the rest of you."

She swallowed hard, and the moment turned to something else. Probably because he was standing there with his jeans and boxers hiked down to R-rated level, and the air and his body were still sizzling.

"Slade?" The voice whipped through the room and sent Maya and him flying even farther apart.

He fixed his jeans and pressed the button on the intercom mounted near the light switch so it would allow Declan to hear him.

"I'm here," Slade told his brother. "What's wrong?" And he figured something had to be wrong for Declan to contact him at this hour.

"A vehicle just triggered the motion detector at the end of the road. No one should be out there."

That was *not* what Slade wanted to hear. He grabbed his gun and hurried to the window. The sun was up, barely, but he couldn't see the end of the road because of the wide curve and some trees.

"I need to get Evan," Maya said on a rise of breath, and she rushed out and back into the other bedroom.

"Stay down and away from the windows," Slade reminded her, but he figured it was unnecessary.

"Backup's been alerted," Declan added. But Slade heard what his brother didn't add. That backup wouldn't be nearly fast enough. "My advice? You've got a couple of minutes before that vehicle reaches you, so you should get the heck out of there."

Slade had already decided the same thing. "We're leaving," he shouted to Maya, and he hurried out of the room, nearly running right into her.

She had Evan in her arms, his bottle, too, and she reached down to grab the diaper bag.

But Slade stopped her.

Even though his mind was racing with the need to escape, he had to consider all angles. The location of the safe house was secret, only known to his brothers, and they wouldn't have told anyone.

"Leave the bag. The plastic one with the formula, too," Slade insisted when she shook her head.

Thankfully, she didn't ask why. Maya just ran with him, first to get the keys and his backup weapon from the coffee table and then to the back door. Slade got them into the truck as fast as possible and drove away.

Even in the dim light he could see that Maya's hands were shaking as she strapped Evan into the car seat. "How did he find us?"

Slade didn't know, and he didn't have time to

answer. He saw the blur of movement in his side mirror. And the glint of sunlight on metal.

"Get down!" he shouted.

Just as the sound of the shot cracked through the air.

## Chapter Nine

Maya threw herself over Evan, and praying, she tried to brace herself for the worst, for the bullet to rip through the truck and into one of them. Thank God that didn't happen. The gunman must have missed.

But he immediately fired off another shot.

Slade cursed but didn't return fire. He kept his gun ready in his right hand, but he slammed his foot on the accelerator.

The road was little more than a dirt path, uneven and littered with potholes. The truck bobbled over the surface, slinging them back and forth. Except for Evan. Somehow, she'd managed to get him buckled in. Maya didn't want to think how bad this could be if she hadn't done that.

Another shot came.

Then another.

She put her hands over Evan's ears to shut out the noise. "Who's trying to kill us?" she asked, not really expecting an answer from Slade.

"He's not shooting at us. He's trying to shoot out the tires."

Mercy, that couldn't happen. Because if the gunman managed to disable the vehicle, he could kidnap Evan. Or at least try. Slade and she would do whatever it took to make sure that didn't happen, but they couldn't risk getting into a gunfight with this man.

Or *men*.

It hit her then. There was no way the driver of the vehicle on the other road could have made it back here ahead of them. So there were two attackers.

Maybe more.

And that sent another jolt of terror through her.

The gunman got off two more shots, but the truck didn't jerk or move as if the tires had been hit. Maya said another prayer of thanks for that and yet another prayer when Slade turned off the trail and onto a road.

"Keep low but try to keep watch," Slade told her. "There could be someone out here waiting for us."

Oh, God. He was right. Whoever was behind these kidnappings was determined to get his or her hands on Evan, but Maya was equally determined to keep her baby safe.

Slade kept watch, too, his gaze slashing back and forth from the side and rearview mirrors. Maya did the same, but she didn't see anyone, only the empty country road. She hoped it stayed that way.

"Any chance someone could have broken into your car and planted a tracking device on Evan's car seat?" Slade asked.

That sent yet another slam of fear through her, and Maya's first reaction was to say no, that there wasn't a chance of something like that happening in Spring Hill. But the first kidnapping attempt had happened there, so she couldn't be sure.

"Where would someone put a device like that?" Maya frantically ran her hands around the seat, lifted it a fraction and felt there, too.

Nothing.

Evan was awake, his eyes trained on Slade again, but she lifted the baby as much as the straps would allow and felt around the padding beneath him.

"Some are as small as a box of matches." Slade glanced over at her search just as Maya looked at him to say she hadn't found anything.

She saw the worry that was no doubt mirrored in her own eyes. But she saw something else. For just a second or two, Slade's expression changed when his gaze landed on Evan. Of course, Maya had already known that he looked at her son with affection, but this was different.

He was looking at Evan as if the baby were *his*.

That didn't help with the adrenaline that was spiking through her. Didn't help with the memories of that kiss that she was trying to forget. That look only made things much, much worse. Because she might be saving Evan only to lose him to the very man who could keep him safe.

"What's wrong?" Slade asked. "Did you find something?"

Maya realized she was staring at him, and she shook her head to answer his question. No, she hadn't found a tracking device, but that look had drilled home something she was terrified to accept.

Slade huffed. Maybe because he was frustrated from the attack. Or from everything else about their situation.

"Don't borrow more trouble," he mumbled.

He didn't add more, because he took the turn off the rural road and onto the one that led to the interstate. At the same time, his phone rang, and he pulled it out and put it on speaker.

"Are you out of the house?" Declan asked the moment Slade answered.

"Yeah. Any idea who just fired shots at us?"

"Not yet, but someone should be out there in the next twenty minutes. If there's anything left to find, we'll find it."

Good. Maya held on to the hope that something would link this to the person behind the attacks and kidnappings.

"What's your situation now?" Declan asked. "Anyone in pursuit?"

Slade checked the mirrors again. "Not that I can tell. But there might be a tracker on one of the items we brought with us. Unless you have some other idea as to how this SOB found us."

"None, but we'll search for the tracker. Where are you now?"

Slade pushed some buttons on the GPS and turned on the ramp to the interstate. Instant traffic. Maya wasn't sure if that was good or bad. Obviously, the shooter knew which vehicle they were in, so even if he wasn't personally in pursuit, that didn't mean he hadn't phoned for help.

"We're about twenty minutes from Maverick Springs," Slade told his brother. "I'm heading to the marshals' office, but I'll need to have someone pick up some supplies for the baby."

Maya blinked. "Aren't the suspects there?"

"They are," Declan confirmed. "Well, Andrea, Nadine and Chase are anyway. Still no sign of Morgan Gambill, the guy who escaped during the bomb scare."

Too bad he was still missing, because Maya figured he had important info. Judging from Slade's scowl, he believed it, too.

"But I do have some news on Randall Martin's missing green SUV," Declan added. "The San Antonio police found it in the parking lot of an abandoned warehouse."

Maya held her breath, hoping this would be the break in the case they needed. But obviously Slade wasn't so hopeful. He looked on the verge of mumbling some profanity. "What's wrong?" he asked his brother.

"Pretty much everything. The person behind the wheel was a thug, Clifford Atwood."

Not Randall, the owner. Maybe he'd been telling the truth about his vehicle being stolen.

"Atwood has a long history of drug-related crimes," Declan added.

Slade repeated the man's name. So did Maya, but it wasn't a name she recognized. "Why would a druggie want to kidnap my son?"

"I think Atwood was just a lackey," Declan explained. "Now he's a dead one. Someone shot him at point-blank range on the left side of his head."

Maya couldn't stop the images from coming. Not images of a man she didn't know but those from her own attack.

It wasn't logical, but violence always brought back memories. Of course, in this case Atwood deserved to die because he'd tried to kidnap Evan. Or worse. The way he'd bashed into her car with the SUV, he could have killed Slade, Evan and her.

Slade's jaw muscles tightened and stirred. "Please tell me there's some evidence in the SUV that points to the missing babies or whoever hired Atwood."

"Nothing," Declan answered right away. "SAPD will keep looking, though. We might get lucky."

Might. But it sounded like a dead end—literally.

"You want me to get started on another safe house?" Declan asked.

Maya groaned softly. They definitely needed a safe place to go, but the thought of being discovered again made her feel sick. She brushed a kiss on Evan's forehead. Then his cheek. And wished she could do more to keep her baby out of this dangerous mess.

"Hold off on the safe house," Slade answered. "I'm thinking about taking them to the ranch."

Even though she couldn't see Declan's face, Maya could feel his surprise. He paused a long time. "Let me know what you decide. I'll see you in a few." And Declan ended the call.

"The ranch?" she challenged. "As in the one you and your brothers run?"

Slade nodded. "Yeah, and I know what you're thinking. The kidnapper will know to look for us there, but it won't be his first choice of places to launch another attack."

Maybe. After all, from what she'd gathered in her internet search, all five of his brothers were marshals and lived at the ranch. It no doubt had some kind of security along with ranch hands who could keep watch for a kidnapper. But there was another side to going there. A bad one.

"Your family could be hurt in an attack."

Slade didn't jump to deny that. "We'll have to take precautions."

He didn't have time to say what those might be, because his phone rang again, and Evan started to fuss. It wasn't time for his bottle, but it was possible he needed a diaper change. Unfortunately, she didn't have any way of doing that. She didn't even have a pacifier, but Maya tried to gently rock the car seat. It didn't help. Evan's whimpers turned to cries.

"We're almost there," Slade let her know. And he took the turn off the highway and toward Maverick Springs.

Probably because her nerves were already at the breaking point, Evan's cries only made it worse. Maya wanted nothing more than to pull him into her arms and try to comfort him, but she couldn't risk taking him from the seat.

It seemed to take an eternity for Slade to turn into the parking lot of the Marshals Service, and the moment they came to a stop, she picked up her baby. He just kept crying.

"I know how you feel, little man," Slade mumbled, and he hooked his arm around both of them to help them from the truck.

And just like that, Evan hushed.

It seemed like such a petty thing, for her to be upset that Evan was responding better to Slade than to her. But it was worse than pettiness. Was Slade's ability to soothe the baby some kind of proof of a genetic connection?

She silently groaned.

*You're losing it.*

Slade got them inside the building and up the stairs, past the reception-security and to the sprawling office that was jammed with desks and cubicles.

And people.

All those people were chatting, and the room was a beehive of activity. But then everything stopped when Slade and she stepped inside.

"Are you okay?" a woman immediately asked. The jeans-wearing blonde rushed toward them, and even though she didn't pull Slade into her arms for a hug, she looked as if that's what she wanted to do.

"We're fine." Slade's tone was slightly warmer than usual, and the woman seemed surprised when Slade brushed his hand over her arm.

The blonde's attention went to Maya, then Evan. "I'm Caitlyn Barnes."

"Maya Ellison."

Caitlyn hitched her thumb in the direction of a wide-shouldered man at one of the desks. "That's Slade's brother Marshal Harlan McKinney, my fiancé."

Maya recalled the name from her internet search and Slade's earlier conversation. Harlan clicked a button on his phone and came closer. His dark eyebrow lifted when his attention landed on Slade's unbuttoned shirt. Only then did Maya realize just how disheveled she probably looked. And maybe he thought that dishevelment wasn't all from the quick escape they'd made from the safe house.

"I've arranged to have formula and diapers delivered," another man said.

"My brother Clayton," Slade clarified. "You remember Declan and that's Wyatt."

Marshal Wyatt McCabe.

If she were putting labels on them, Harlan looked like a pro-football linebacker. Declan, a rodeo rider. Clayton, a jeans-wearing lawyer. Slade, a vampire and not one with friendly intentions, either. But Wyatt, well, his looks seemed more like the kind a lead singer in a rock band would have. Except his clothes were pure cowboy. He even wore his gun in an old-fashioned hip holster.

Wyatt's mouth bent as if he might smile, but when he looked at Evan, the smile went south. He mumbled something about it being nice to meet her and strolled out.

"Does he have a problem with me?" Maya whispered to Slade.

He glanced at Wyatt, who was disappearing down the hall. "No. It's the baby. Wyatt's always wanted to be a father, and he hired a surrogate but something went wrong with the deal, I think. Nothing that he's ready to talk about, though."

She gathered that wasn't usual. Probably because they were family and discussed their lives with each other, but judging from Wyatt's sullen reaction, something more than just *wrong* had happened.

"It doesn't help that the ranch is going through a mini baby boom," Clayton said, taking up the explanation. "My son is due any day now. And our other brother, Dallas, and his wife, Joelle, are expecting."

Maya glanced at their faces and then around the room. "They all believe Evan's your son?"

Slade did some glancing, too. "Probably."

There it was. That unruffled response she was starting to know so well. But his answer didn't need the heavy emotion for it to hit her hard. If Evan was indeed his child, Slade would have plenty of moral support. He had a family already in place to help him win a custody battle.

Something she didn't.

Slade hesitated a moment. Looked down at Evan. "Come on."

He led her down the hall where Wyatt had disappeared minutes earlier. They passed several rooms, all with the doors closed, and she figured their suspects were in those rooms. Nadine and Chase Collier. Andrea, too. The two people who weren't there were Randall Martin and Morgan Gambill, but Maya hoped that with Slade's entire family seemingly working on this, it wouldn't be long before they could bring them in.

And get answers.

Of course, those answers were just the beginning.

Stopping the danger was a must. Finding the missing babies, too. Then she'd have to deal with the results of the DNA test Slade had ordered.

Slade took her into what appeared to be a break room and had her sit in one of the chairs. "It won't be long before the diapers and formula arrive." His stare stayed fixed on Evan for several long moments.

Maya also looked at her son, to try to see what Slade was seeing. "Does he look like Deidre?" But she didn't want to hear any answer other than *no*.

"Truth is, I don't know. I never saw a picture of Deidre as a baby. Nor one of me, either. And I have no idea who my birth parents were. My mother was supposedly an addict and a prostitute who sneaked out of the hospital right after I was born."

Maya pulled in her breath. That sort of thing probably happened all the time, but it tugged at her heart to know that Slade's start in life had begun at what was essentially rock bottom.

"Your adopted parents didn't take pictures of you?" Because she'd already taken dozens of Evan and couldn't imagine an adoptive parent who wouldn't do the same.

"My adoption was…complicated." He sank down in the chair beside her and rubbed his index finger over the back of Evan's hand. Her son's eyes were already drifting down, but he opened them and stared at Slade. "I was given to a family when I was a couple of months old, but before the adoption was final, the woman got cancer and died. I ended up with another family. Then another."

She'd been a victims' rights advocate long enough to know that probably meant Slade had been removed from an abusive environment.

"I don't remember a lot of it," he said as if he knew exactly what she was thinking. "And by the time I was old enough to remember, I was strong enough to fight back."

That created more of a tug in her heart. No child should have to fight back anyone or anything.

"And then you landed in Rocky Creek Children's Facility," she mumbled.

He nodded, but other than a flex of his jaw muscles, he had no reaction. She was betting inside, though, he had enough bad memories to last a lifetime or two. Thankfully, Kirby Granger had rescued him, and if Kirby had had to kill Jonah Webb to do that, then maybe it was justified.

Maya winced at that thought.

Until now, until this whole ordeal, she'd never thought of violence as justified. Still, maybe it had been in that case. And it was certainly warranted if it would keep Evan safe.

"At least Kirby gave you a home," Maya said.

But he didn't jump to agree with her. "He gave me the attention a father gives a son. And he made me a part of the ranch."

No mention of family. "He gave you your brothers," Maya reminded him.

"Yeah." And he hesitated again. "For the record, I didn't kill Deidre's lover," Slade volunteered. "The guy committed suicide before he could tell the cops what he'd done with Deidre's baby."

That ate away at her, too. Maya prayed the man hadn't done anything to hurt the newborn. Of course, maybe the only reason she had Evan was because this now-dead man had taken his estranged lover's child that she'd conceived with Slade.

"Good thing he killed himself," Slade said under his breath. "Because after seeing what he'd done to Deidre, there's no way I could have held myself back."

Maya swallowed hard, and though she knew this would complicate the heck out of things, she leaned over and brushed a kiss on Slade's cheek. It seemed far more intimate than the scalding-hot kiss they'd shared in the bedroom at the safe house. More dangerous, too.

Because she was falling for him.

And that couldn't happen.

"Flashbacks?" he asked. Maya must have looked as confused as she felt, because he added, "You made a face after you kissed me. I figured maybe it was causing flashbacks."

Of her attack.

She understood then. Slade probably thought any

intimacy would trigger flashbacks. Probably should have, too. It had the couple of times she'd tried to go on dates. But with Slade it hadn't been flashbacks and nightmarish memories going through her head.

That didn't make her feel better.

Just the opposite.

"Oh," he mumbled, and he had a split-second smile. He probably didn't know he had a killer smile to go along with those killer good looks.

"I don't want to want you," she let him know.

Slade nodded. "Ditto." His gaze met hers. "You're the worst kind of complication. The kind that could cause me to lose focus. And I never lose focus."

It sounded as if he was trying to convince himself. Or maybe it was just a reminder. Either way, she didn't feel herself pulling away from him. Maya leaned against him, her arm pressed to his, knowing it was a mistake but not doing anything to correct it.

And that's how Declan found them when he appeared in the doorway.

Slade and she eased away from each other, but coupled with the fact that Slade had shown up with an unbuttoned shirt, Declan probably thought Slade and she were well on their way to becoming lovers. Or already had.

Declan came into the room and set down a bag near her chair. The diapers and formula, no doubt.

"The Colliers' lawyer is here," Declan told his brother. He handed Slade some papers. "That's the background check on them."

Slade glanced over the pages, scowled.

"Yeah," his brother verified. Obviously, Declan had read it, too. "We're not looking at parents of the year here."

Maya wasn't sure what had caused Declan to say that, but she hoped she got a chance to read the background check that had created Slade's scowl.

"Andrea's lawyer is here, too," Declan added, "so we can start the interviews."

Good. Maybe one of them would confess and this would be over soon.

Slade and Declan's gazes stayed locked. "What's wrong?" Slade asked.

Maya's head whipped up, and even though she hardly knew Declan, she saw it then. The troubled look in his eyes.

"I had someone go through the safe house," Declan explained, "and they found a GPS tracking device. That's how the kidnapper knew where to find you."

Maya adjusted Evan in her arms and slowly rose to her feet. "So the house wasn't safe after all."

Declan shook his head. "The house was fine, but the GPS device was in the plastic grocery bag you'd brought with you. Where did you get the bag?"

Maya groaned. "From Sheriff Monroe."

Declan scrubbed his hand over his face, cursed. "I'll get him out here so we can question him."

## Chapter Ten

Yet one more thing to add to the list—make sure Sheriff Monroe hadn't aided and abetted the kidnapper by placing a tracking device in the bag he'd given Maya and Slade. He figured the sheriff was innocent, that someone else had planted the bug, but the whole mess would have to be cleared up.

Along with the other messes on the ever-growing list.

First and foremost was keeping Evan and Maya safe, but the missing babies were equally important. After all, one of those baby boys might be his son, and even if they weren't, if Evan was his child, Slade still wanted the babies back safe and sound.

Declan's phone buzzed, and he stepped back into the hall to answer it.

Evan's whimpers pulled Slade from his thoughts, and he checked the time. The baby was probably hungry, wet or both, and while the marshals' building wasn't the most convenient place to tend to a baby's needs, it was safe.

Well, hopefully.

After everything else that'd happened, he wasn't letting Maya and Evan out of his sight. Unfortunately, that meant they were stuck there until he or one of his brothers had interviewed their suspects.

"I need one of the diapers," she told Slade. She set the bottle she'd brought with them on the floor next to the chair. "And wipes if there are any in the bag."

There were, which made him suspect that his very pregnant sister-in-law, Lenora, had been the one to buy the items. He seriously doubted any of his brothers would know to include such things.

Maya repositioned Evan on her lap so that his feet were against her stomach, and she pulled open the blanket. He wasn't sure how she managed it, but she unsnapped the stretchy blue one-piece outfit and changed Evan's diaper. Evan wasn't happy about the maneuvering, though, because his cries got louder.

"I have to warm the formula," Maya said, tipping her head to the microwave on the counter. She glanced around as if trying to figure out how to accomplish that.

Slade solved the problem for her. He scooped Evan into his arms. Like the night before, he got that punch of emotion and something he rarely felt.

Peace.

Yeah, he was surrounded by family. Five brothers and a foster father he'd take a bullet for. But truth was, he'd never felt as much of a part of the family as the others obviously did. Maybe because they'd figured out a way to put their pasts behind them.

Something Slade had never quite managed.

For the first time, it felt, well, possible.

What would it be like to be a father to his child? To any child? To have that unconditional love that he hadn't experienced from anyone but Kirby? It was something he'd never allowed himself to consider.

But he considered it now.

If Evan was his, then he might have to consider joint custody. Or something. He couldn't just rip this baby from Maya's life.

And that made him one sick puppy.

Because he was thinking with his heart now, and he was pretty sure that wouldn't send him down the best path. Nope. In addition to the distraction it'd cause, it might become the worst hurt of his life.

Maya cleared her throat, and when Slade looked up at her, she had her attention fastened not on Evan but on the hall. He looked past Declan, who was still on the phone, and saw the blond-haired couple making a beeline toward them.

Slade recognized them from their photos—Nadine and Chase Collier. The tall dark-haired guy in a suit behind them was no doubt their lawyer. Slade automatically stood and handed Maya the baby so he could put his hand over the butt of his gun.

"Marshal Becker?" Nadine asked. There was nothing friendly about her tone. Or her eyes. Ice-blue, the same color as the body-hugging skirt and top she was wearing. Everything about her screamed trophy wife, including the fact that she was nearly twenty years younger than her husband.

Declan ended his call and would have stepped between the Colliers and them, but Slade did the stepping first. He moved into the doorway so that he was in front of Maya and the baby.

"I'm Becker," Slade let her know.

He hadn't thought it possible but Nadine's ice-blue eyes narrowed even more. She had on so much makeup that he was surprised her lashes didn't gunk together.

"You're the one accusing us of stealing our own child," she snapped.

Chase didn't acknowledge her comment, but he did extend his hand. Slade shook it, eventually.

"Marshal, we're hoping you have a lead on our son's kidnapper," Chase said to Slade.

It wasn't just his tone that made him seem different from his wife. The Colliers were definitely an odd couple. Chase looked more like an aging rocker with his cargo pants, black T-shirt and spiked blond hair. Plus, there was the nose ring. Slade wasn't opposed to body piercings and such, but on Chase it made him look like a man who was clinging to his youth.

And failing miserably at it.

"I was hoping you had a lead," Slade fired back.

"See?" Nadine grumbled. "He thinks we took Will." She folded her arms over her ample chest. "Why in the name of God would you believe we'd do that?"

Slade lifted his shoulder. "People do all sorts of things for reasons that don't make sense to me. Like gambling, for instance." He waited because he figured that would strike a nerve.

It did.

Nadine cursed him, but Chase only huffed. "My wife has control issues," he volunteered. "She loves flying to Vegas and dropping a bundle of my money." Chase paused, his mud-brown eyes fixed on Slade. "But, of course, you're referring to the questionable loans she took out to try to hide her debts from me."

"My debts have nothing to do with this." Nadine jabbed her perfectly manicured index finger at Slade. "And I resent the implication. If you want to accuse someone of stealing Will, then look at Chase."

Slade did indeed look at the man, but Chase was now glaring at his wife. "Nadine gets things mixed up in her head. She seems to believe I'd steal Will to punish her. But there's one problem with that. Nadine didn't want a child to begin with. The only reason she agreed was because she thought it would stop me from divorcing her. It won't."

"And if you think I'll just hand you a divorce,

then think again," Nadine fired back. "There was no prenup, which means I'm entitled to half of the Collier estate. Besides, you cheated on me, and I'm betting I can convince a judge to give me a lot more than half."

Chase moved in so close to his wife that he was practically in her face. "Prove the cheating." His mouth twisted in a sick smile. "Oh, but you can't, can you? Maybe because you were too busy climbing between the sheets with the pool boy or that dealer in Vegas."

Oh, man. Under the definition of toxic marriage, there was probably a picture of those two clowns. Slade had spent just minutes with them and wanted to knock some sense into both of them.

"I didn't take Will," Slade heard someone say a split second before he saw the speaker. It was Andrea, and she was making a beeline for them.

Great. Now the gang was all here. Their lawyers, too, since Andrea's was trailing along right behind her.

"Why don't we just make this easy on everyone?" Slade suggested. "One of you just confess so we can get those babies to a safe place."

He watched their reactions.

Nadine started to howl about her innocence. Andrea began crying again. And Chase's attention went over Slade's shoulder and to Evan. Chase might have even gone over to Evan if Slade hadn't stepped in front of the man.

Chase shook his head as if pulling himself out of a trance. "Sorry. He just reminds me of Will."

There was the emotion that Slade had been looking for.

Maybe it was genuine. Maybe not.

But at least Chase appeared to be the concerned father of a missing child. Andrea was making a show of being the wrongfully accused, worried nanny. The only one of the lot who was spouting the poor-pitiful-me act was Nadine.

Slade glanced back at Maya. She was standing, feeding Evan his bottle, but he also saw the weariness in her eyes. It'd already been a hellishly long day, and he wanted to cut this little visit short so he could make plans to get them out of there.

He turned to Nadine, though it put a knot in his gut just to look at her. "Give me your best guess as to who took Will."

Nadine blinked, maybe because she hadn't expected the direct question. "If I knew, I'd tell you. Just because I didn't want a child, it doesn't mean I want Will to get hurt."

Okay. More of what he was looking for. At this point he'd take even fake emotion.

Slade turned to Andrea, who was staring at Nadine. "I think she took Will and hid him somewhere," Andrea said.

Nadine huffed. "If I'd done that, I damn sure wouldn't have burned down the house." Her gaze came back to Slade. "Any idea how long it'll take me to replace all the things that fire destroyed?"

Slade didn't even attempt to answer that, because it would require him to get his jaw unlocked. Instead he looked at Chase. "Give me the name of the person you suspect."

"Nadine," he said without hesitation.

So two votes for Nadine, and she was looking like a top suspect in his eyes, too.

"Well, I suspect you!" Nadine fired back at her husband. She whirled around toward Slade. "And he'll claim he doesn't have motive, but he does. If he can get me locked up for kidnapping, it'll save him millions because he won't have to pay up when I divorce him."

Slade groaned. His head was starting to throb, and it only proved what he already knew. All three of them were suspects.

"Who's interviewing them?" Slade asked Declan.

"Harlan's taking the Colliers, and Wyatt will be with Andrea."

Good choices. Harlan was big and intimidating. Not that intimidation would work on Nadine, but Harlan had a poker player's patience, and he could maybe spur them into an incriminating argument. And as for Andrea, well, Wyatt was a first-class charmer, so perhaps he could work his magic on the young woman.

"This way," Declan told the trio, and he got them moving back to their respective interview rooms.

"You okay?" Slade asked Maya, and because she looked ready to collapse, he took her by the arm.

"Please tell me when you find that baby, you won't give him back to those people."

It was a promise he had no trouble keeping. "The adoption isn't final, and I'll make sure it never is."

Maya was no doubt thinking he'd do the same to her if he found out Evan was his. Soon they were going to have to talk about that.

Once Declan had deposited their suspects in the interview rooms, Slade motioned for his brother to come back to the break room. He had a plan, but he couldn't do it alone.

"I need a decoy vehicle," he explained to Declan. "Because I'm pretty sure that the kidnapper has a hired gun who'll try to follow us."

And now here was the hard part. Slade turned to Maya. "I want Declan and my brother's fiancée, Caitlyn, to take the baby to the ranch."

"No," Maya said before he could even finish. She pulled Evan closer to her.

"It's the safest thing for Evan." Yeah, that was playing dirty, but it was true. "You and I'll leave together, and you'll pretend to be carrying Evan in your arms."

Slade wished he had a way to keep Maya out of this, but the kidnapper's lackey would zoom in on her, figuring that wherever she went, so would the baby.

"What if the kidnapper comes after Declan and Caitlyn?" she asked.

"They'll leave out back at the exact moment we leave through the front. The kidnapper will want us followed."

As Slade had expected, tears shimmered in her eyes. "But how long will I be away from Evan?"

"Not long." He hoped. "We'll have to drive around until we lose this guy, and then I'll take you back to the ranch."

"The kidnapper will guess that's where we're going."

"Even if he does, he might not want to go barreling onto the ranch with my brothers. Declan, Dallas and Clayton will all be there. Plus the ranch hands."

Maya was still shaking her head, and those tears were now spilling down her cheeks.

"I'll get things ready," Declan said. He scribbled something on a piece of paper and handed it to Slade before he walked away: "Distract her."

Declan had no doubt noticed those tears and probably thought Maya was about to bolt. She wasn't. But that didn't mean Declan's tactics were wrong. A distraction might help. Well, with the tears anyway.

"I hate feeling this way." Maya's voice was a hoarse whisper.

Slade touched his fingers to her waist, urged her closer. "You're scared. And you hate having to rely on me."

Her forehead bunched up. Clearly, she wasn't pleased he knew that about her or with his attempt to distract her.

He brushed a kiss on her temple. "Don't worry. Soon you can rely on yourself again."

She didn't say anything, but he wished he had a way of reading her mind. Because this time, he couldn't figure out what was going on in her head. There was something in her expression. A different kind of fear, maybe. Or else he was just projecting his own fear.

"For the record, I'm not used to relying on anybody, either," he let her know.

She huffed. "You're not relying on anyone now. Certainly not me."

"Wrong." He shook his head and tapped his temple. "You're here now. I don't want you there, and I'm pretty sure you feel the same."

"I do," she readily admitted. But she, too, shook her head. "I can't get involved with you like that, Slade."

"Yeah." He leaned in, brushed his mouth over hers and felt the kick of heat when her breath shuddered against his lips.

"*Yeah* as in you agree?" she asked.

"*Like that* as in sex?" he countered.

No answer was necessary, because they both knew they were just blowing smoke with this conversation. Both were hell-bent on stopping something that it wasn't in their power to stop. He didn't believe in soul mates or love at first sight, but Slade did believe in basic attraction.

Slade moved in closer, put his mouth to her ear. "Sooner or later this pull between us will make it darn near impossible to remember just how bad this'll screw things up."

Maya pulled back, swallowed hard, but she didn't move away when Slade kissed her again.

"That's your idea of a distraction?" someone mumbled.

Slade snapped in the direction of the speaker and saw Declan just a few feet away. Hell. Slade hadn't even heard his little brother's approach.

Maya wasn't the only one in distraction mode.

"The vehicles are almost ready," Declan said, thankfully not lingering on the kiss he'd just witnessed. "And I spoke with Sheriff Monroe. He claims he didn't put a tracking device in the bag. His wife picked up the formula and diapers, and she says she didn't do it, either."

"Well, someone sure as heck did," Slade snarled.

Declan mumbled an agreement. "That's why I faxed the sheriff a photo of Clifford Atwood, the dead guy we found behind the wheel of the SUV used to attack you. The sheriff's wife says she's almost positive she saw him in the grocery store when she was shopping for the baby things."

"But how could he have managed to put the GPS in the bag without her noticing?" Maya asked.

Slade didn't have any trouble coming up with an answer. A plausible one that could mean both the sheriff and his wife were innocent. "Atwood could have bumped into her and dropped it into the bag. Atwood was a career criminal, so it probably wouldn't have been much of a challenge to do something like this. Especially since the sheriff's wife was likely in a hurry."

"What about fingerprints?" Maya asked. "Were there any on the GPS?"

Declan shook his head. "Nothing. No prints or trace. But we might get something from the area around the safe house. The CSIs out there found footprints along the trail where the guy took shots at you. Spent casings, too."

And sometimes fingerprints could be recovered from those. Any prints could lead them to the hired guns, which in turn could lead them to the kidnapper.

Declan glanced around as if making sure no one was close enough to hear what he had to say. "There's a truck out back, and I figure that's the way Caitlyn, Dallas and I will leave with the baby—

minus the blanket you have him wrapped in. You can stuff that blanket with something and leave through the front of the building with Clayton. I've had Evan's car seat moved to the vehicle you'll be taking so if anyone is watching, they'll believe you really have the baby with you. We have another car seat in the truck thanks to Clayton and Lenora."

"Get Caitlyn," Slade said before Maya had a chance to change her mind about this plan. And before he had a chance to change his.

Declan turned, but he only made it one step before he stopped in his tracks. He didn't draw his gun, but he did put his hand over it, and Slade did the same.

"What's wrong?" Maya asked. Thankfully, she moved behind him, because Slade's attention was on the man who'd just stepped into the hall.

A man he recognized from photos. And a man he very much wanted to see. Just not with Maya and Evan around.

Their suspect Randall Martin.

*Chapter Eleven*

It took several heart-slamming moments before Maya could see the man who'd caused Slade and Declan to go on full alert. And even after seeing him she had no idea who he was until Slade mumbled his name like profanity.

Randall Martin.

Declan took out his phone and pressed some buttons. "We just got a visitor. How the heck did he get in, and was he armed when he went through the metal detector?"

She couldn't hear the answer, but Declan looked at Slade, shook his head and put his phone away. "The dispatcher's new, and when Randall said he was a visitor, she processed him through. He didn't set off the alarms, but he could have some kind of nonmetal weapon on him."

"I don't. I carry a gun, usually concealed, and yes, I have a permit to do that," Randall volunteered. "But I left it in my car. Didn't figure I should give you boys any more reason for concern."

"We've been looking for you," Slade said. His voice was all lawman, and there was zero trace of the heat that had been there just seconds earlier.

"I heard." Randall walked closer, and she got a better look at him. Late thirties, pasty white skin and hair that seemed way too black to be natural. He wore an expensive-looking linen suit, not at all what she'd expected from the owner of a bowling alley. Judging from the clothes, the business was very successful.

"I also heard that you plan to accuse me of trying to kill you," Randall added. He was a big man, even bigger than Slade, and he met their stony glare with one of his own. "I didn't." He reached in his pocket, causing both Declan and Slade to draw their guns.

Randall rolled his eyes in a dramatic fashion. "It's a copy of the surveillance footage from the parking lot of the bowling alley." He pulled out a disk and offered it to Slade.

Slade took it, but he didn't reholster his gun as Declan did.

"When you watch the footage," Randall went on, "you'll see that I was telling the truth about someone stealing my SUV. It's not my primary vehicle. I use it mainly for employees to do pick-ups and deliveries, so I didn't notice it missing right away."

Declan and Slade exchanged glances before Slade looked back at her. "Stay behind me."

She had no intention of facing this man head-on,

not with Evan in her arms. They went up the hall to an office, Slade staying between Randall and her, but that didn't stop the man from peering around Slade to look first at her.

Then at Evan.

"Glad he's safe," Randall told her. "I'll bet this has you rattled. Sorry about that, but I didn't have anything to do with it."

Maya wasn't certain she believed him. Judging from Slade's body language, neither did he.

Declan put the disk into a laptop on the desk in the office, and it didn't take long before the images appeared on the screen. A dimly lit parking lot at night with only two vehicles—a BMW and the green SUV. She could see the neon sign for the Perfect Strike bowling alley.

"Fast-forward to just past midnight," Randall instructed. "The place was closed, but I was still there working in my office."

Declan moved the footage to midnight, and a man appeared on the screen. He walked—no, he skulked—from the back of the building and straight to the SUV. She couldn't see the device he used to unlock the door, but it took him only a few seconds to get in.

"I don't use my car alarms," Randall explained. "I got tired of having to turn them off when someone would accidentally trip it just by getting too close.

Wish it'd been on in this case, though, so I could have caught this moron."

Declan zoomed in on the car thief's face, and even with the grainy texture of the footage, Maya had no trouble recognizing the guy.

"Clifford Atwood," Slade and she mumbled in unison.

Of course, they'd known Atwood had been in the vehicle because he'd been found dead behind the wheel. She also didn't have any trouble believing Atwood had attacked them.

Or rather had been hired to attack them.

"Atwood has a connection to Nadine Collier." Randall paused and looked a little smug after tossing that out there. "I'm sure you would have found it soon enough, but I hired several P.I.s to get to the bottom of this. And to do something else," he added in a mumble. The smugness vanished, and he didn't volunteer any more about that "something else."

"What connection?" Slade snapped.

"He was her bookie for a lot of her horse betting. And I'd rather not say how I came by this information, but if you ask around, you'll eventually find someone who'll squeal."

Declan cursed. "But not you?"

Randall gave him a flat look. "Someone put a bullet in Atwood's head, and I'd rather not meet the same fate."

Maya couldn't fault him for that, but Randall

was holding something back. "You think Atwood and Nadine are connected to the kidnappings?" she asked.

He shifted his position so that he could better see her. But he didn't answer. He looked at Evan again, squeezed his eyes shut and groaned.

"I don't know about Atwood and Nadine," Randall finally said. His attention shifted to Slade. "But I got something to tell you that's going to make me look guilty."

Maya certainly hadn't expected that, and she held her breath, waiting.

"My girlfriend, Gina Blackwell, and I split up a few months ago." He paused again, cleared his throat. "She was pregnant, and I told her when she had the baby to contact me. If the kid turned out to be mine, I was more than willing to pay child support. But she didn't call me. I found out a few days ago that she'd delivered a baby boy."

Oh, mercy. Maya didn't like where this appeared to be going.

Slade eased his gun back in his holster. "Are you saying one of the kidnapped adopted babies is your son?"

Randall dragged in a long, weary breath. "It's possible. That's why I hired the P.I.s. I've been looking for both Gina and the baby, but then I just found out this morning that Gina had given the child up for adoption."

"How'd you learn that?" Slade pressed.

He handed Slade a business card that he took from his pocket. "From a waitress friend of Gina's. Her name and contact info are on the back of the card. According to this woman, she and Gina worked together, and she was with Gina when she went into labor. She claims she drove Gina to the hospital but that both Gina and the baby were gone when she went back later to check on them." Randall stopped again. "I'm pretty sure the birth date of Gina's kid matches those of the kidnapped babies. And *him.*"

Maya dropped back a step when Randall's gaze snapped to Evan. She pulled the bottle from her son's mouth and put him against her chest and shoulder so that Randall couldn't see his face.

"You have a strong motive to be the kidnapper," Maya managed to say.

The anger was instant, and it shot through Randall's already dark eyes. "Would I have told you all of this if I was guilty of kidnapping those babies?" He groaned again, scrubbed his hand over his face. "Besides, Gina might not have even been pregnant with my kid. She slept around a lot."

"Any chance Gina ever used a fake name? Like maybe Crystal Hanson?" Slade asked.

Randall shook his head. "I don't think so."

Despite the dread and fear rushing through her, that gave Maya some hope. Maybe Evan wasn't

Randall's. Or Slade's, for that matter. Maybe when the danger was over, no one but she would have a claim to this child whom she loved more than life itself.

"Who would have known any details about Gina's baby?" Slade asked.

"I don't know. But I intend to find out. Finding Gina and the baby is the fastest way to clear my name. That's why I need your help." Randall tipped his head to the business card he'd given Slade. "My numbers are on there. Call me the second you find out anything."

Randall started to walk out but then stopped. "May I leave, or do you plan to arrest me?"

Slade met him eye-to-eye. "No plans. *Yet.*"

The anger returned to Randall's eyes, but Maya only saw a flash of that before he strolled away.

"I'll call in some favors to get someone started on finding Gina Blackwell," Declan said. He looked at her. "You need to get the baby ready to leave."

Just like that, it felt as if her heart were being crushed in her chest, and she might not have been able to move if Slade hadn't helped her. He led her by the arm back to the break room, and together they took the blanket off Evan. Slade wrapped him in a jacket that he took from the closet.

And he kissed Evan's cheek.

Just as a father would kiss his son.

That crushed her heart, too, not just because

Slade was obviously growing closer to Evan. But because Maya was already starting to spin a fantasy that shouldn't be spun. Of Slade and she raising Evan together.

As a family.

It was a dangerous fantasy, and she reminded herself that Slade could crush her dream world by being Evan's father and taking him from her.

Just as he was doing now.

He eased Evan from her arms when his brothers Declan, Clayton and Dallas and then Caitlyn came into the room.

"Harlan and Wyatt are still doing the interviews," Clayton let them know. "They'll call us if they get anything."

That was a glimmer of good news in what would be a horrible next few minutes. Maybe even hours, since Maya had no idea how long it would take them to get to the ranch.

"I'll take good care of him, I promise," Caitlyn said softly to her.

Maya hated trusting these strangers with her baby's safety, but there were few choices here. They couldn't live at the marshals' office, and this way they might even catch the kidnapper. After all, this was essentially a trap.

Slade took Evan's blanket and grabbed another jacket from the closet. Maya didn't have time for a long goodbye. Just a kiss and a prayer before Slade handed Evan over to Caitlyn and put the blanket and jacket in her arms. Maya used the two items to make the fake baby.

"Move fast and keep watch," Slade said to Declan. "We'll do the same."

"The windows of the vehicles are bullet resistant," Slade told her. He took her arm again and headed to the front of the building. Clayton followed along right behind them.

Maya tried to give Evan one last look but she couldn't see him, because the coat was wrapped around him. Slade led her down the stairs and to the door. He looked out, his lawman's eyes combing over the area before they went outside. They moved fast to the black four-door car. Clayton got behind the wheel, and Slade and she climbed into the backseat.

"Pretend you're strapping the baby into the car seat," Slade instructed.

Somehow Maya got her hands to move, and she put the bundle into the seat as Clayton sped away.

And the waiting and watching began.

She glanced around but didn't see Declan and the others. That probably wouldn't happen until they reached the ranch.

Without taking his attention off their surroundings, Slade reached over and slid his hand around the back of her neck. It was such a simple gesture, but it gave her far more comfort than it should have.

Clayton's phone buzzed, and while he took the call, he drove them out of town. Maya tried to make sense of the nightmare. She wanted to think about anything but Evan and how much she missed him.

"I feel lost without him," she mumbled, looking at the empty car seat.

"Yeah." Slade gave her a quick glance, and she realized it wasn't just a response. It was the truth. In this short period of time, he'd become attached to Evan. Maybe even more than attached. He might even love her son. Maya knew that was possible because she'd loved Evan the first time she'd seen him.

Clayton kept driving, taking one turn right after the other while he talked on the phone that he had sandwiched between his ear and shoulder. Each car around them got Slade's attention. Hers, too, but no vehicle seemed to be following them as they meandered away from town.

"That was the initial report on Gina Blackwell," Clayton relayed to them the moment he ended the call. "She's twenty-four, a waitress and she worked at Randall's bowling alley until about four months ago, but she's been off the radar since."

"Any confirmation that she was pregnant?" Slade asked.

"Yeah. She used one of those free medical clinics, so her name's in the database. She was seeing an obstetrician, but he didn't deliver the baby. Saul's sending someone over there now to try to get her records and interview the doc. Her former coworkers, too."

"Saul Warner," Slade explained to her. "Our boss. You talked to him on the phone yesterday."

She remembered. Maybe the head marshal would get somewhere, but she knew from experience that doctors were often bound by law and privacy acts. Still, they might learn something they could use to find the woman.

"You think Randall was lying about being the kidnapper?" she asked.

Slade lifted his shoulder. "He could have volunteered all that info about his ex just so he wouldn't look guilty."

Yes, and maybe he faked his lack of emotion for the child who might be his. Randall had certainly seemed more concerned about clearing his name than finding the babies.

Clayton continued to drive, and even though he didn't have on the GPS, Maya sensed they were circling Maverick Springs. The minutes just crawled by, but no car came into view. Which meant their plan had failed. The kidnapper hadn't come after them.

"Maybe the kidnapper went after Evan," she mumbled.

"No," he quickly assured her. "Declan would have called us if that'd happened."

The words had no sooner left his mouth than

his phone rang, and her heart slammed against her chest. Maya moved closer, trying to hear what the caller was saying. Thankfully, the call was short, and as soon as he finished it, Slade turned to her.

"They made it safely to the ranch."

The relief was instant and overwhelming, and even though Slade didn't make a sound, his fingers tensed slightly on the back of her neck, reminding her that he was there. Of course, she hadn't needed such a reminder. Slade had a way of making sure his presence was known.

Clayton took several more turns, both Slade and he checking the mirrors, but no one was following them when he made the turn for the Blue Creek Ranch. Maya had been worried about going to Slade's home. Like walking into the lion's den. But now that Evan was there, she couldn't wait to arrive.

The place was huge, with acres of pastures still green despite it being late fall. They passed by two houses; one looked decades old and the other was much newer.

"Harlan and Caitlyn live there." Slade tipped his head to the older house. "Dallas and his wife, Joelle, live in the other. Clayton and Lenora's house is on the back part of the property."

"How secure are the grounds?" she asked.

"The ranch hands are keeping watch for anyone.

Plus, we've moved Lenora to the main house with my foster father, Kirby."

Lenora, the pregnant sister-in-law, and Kirby, who was apparently battling cancer. Maya hated that both could be in danger, and she prayed all the security measures would be enough to keep everyone safe.

Clayton pulled into a circular drive and stopped directly in front of the sprawling house. Maya didn't wait for Slade. She got out and practically ran up the porch steps to the front door. It was locked, but before she could ring the bell, Slade came up from behind her and punched in some numbers on the keypad.

The moment she was inside, Maya heard the voices, and she followed them through the foyer and toward the back of the house to the huge eat-in kitchen. She immediately spotted Declan, Caitlyn and another man wearing a badge.

But Evan wasn't there.

"The baby's upstairs with Stella," Caitlyn jumped to say, probably because Maya looked on the verge of panicking.

"Stella?" That wasn't a name she'd heard before.

"A friend of the family," Slade supplied. "This way." He led her to some back stairs and to the second floor.

There seemed to be dozens of rooms, but Slade took her to one toward the center. A woman with graying auburn hair was standing in front of a crib, and she put her finger to her mouth in a be-quiet gesture.

Stella, no doubt.

Maya probably made more noise than the woman wanted when she raced to the crib. She wanted to scoop him into her arms and kiss him, but Evan was sound asleep, snuggled beneath a pale blue blanket.

"He was just tuckered out," Stella whispered. She smiled when she looked at Maya. "You appear to be, too. I'm Stella Doyle."

"Maya Ellison." She shook hands with the woman. "You have children of your own?" Because she'd obviously done a good job putting Evan to bed. Her baby was on his side and with nothing near his face to interfere with his breathing.

Stella shook her head, and some kind of pained look went through her eyes. "Wasn't blessed with ones of my own, but I did enough of caring for this lot when they were at Rocky Creek. I was the cook there."

The horrible place where Slade had been raised. But apparently she hadn't been responsible for any of that horror or she wouldn't be here. Yet more family. And Maya was beginning to feel as if she was up against an entire united clan who could challenge her for custody of Evan.

Stella hitched her thumb to the king-size bed on the opposite side of the room. "You could probably do with a nap yourself. If you need to freshen up a bit, you'll find everything you need in the bathroom. The housekeeper, Loretta, keeps this room all fixed up for guests."

Obviously, guests with children. Maya hadn't expected the ranch to even have a crib, but she was thankful for it. Especially since she wasn't sure how long they'd be staying.

Hopefully not long.

Stella's attention landed on Slade when he slipped his arm around Maya's waist and looked down at Evan. The woman made a soft sound of surprise and gave Slade's arm a gentle pat.

"Never figured fatherhood would settle this good on you." Stella didn't wait for Slade to say anything. She walked out and eased the door shut behind her.

"I'm sure Stella can get some extra clothes and baby supplies for Evan and you." Slade kept his gaze nailed to Evan and his voice at a whisper.

That was good to know, but it was Stella's fatherhood comment that Maya needed to discuss.

"No," Slade said before she could utter a word.

Maya's eyebrow lifted, challenging that he didn't know what she'd been about to say.

"I didn't bring Evan here so I could shut you out," Slade clarified.

Oh. So he'd known what was racing like wildfire through her head. "But you have so many people on your side."

He still had his arm around her and pulled her closer until she was right against him. "There's only one side here, and it belongs to him." He glanced down at Evan.

It was the perfect thing to say to lessen her fears, and that was a Texas-size red flag. "Careful," she mumbled, "or you'll really lose your bad-boy image."

The corner of his mouth lifted, and she felt the jolt of that blasted smile again. If Slade knew just how much it weakened her defenses and made her go all warm, he would probably use it more often.

But she rethought that.

Slade didn't need to do anything to make her go all warm, and he wasn't a man to resort to tricks to seduce a woman. She came up on her toes, intending to give him a quick brush of her lips. But he made a rumbling sound deep within his throat, turned and snapped her to him.

Definitely not a touch of lips.

He put his mouth to hers and kissed her as only Slade could do. Gently but somehow thoroughly at the same time. And the kiss was just for starters. The taste of him slid through her, easing away all the stress caused by the danger and revving up a different kind of tension.

Sizzling heat.

Before she'd met Slade, it'd been so long since she'd been in a man's arms, and this particular man's arms felt as if they were right where she belonged. Against his body, too, and Slade made sure she could feel every last inch of him when he repositioned her, bringing her breasts against his chest.

"If this makes you feel like panicking, let me know," he mumbled before he took her mouth again.

It took her a moment to cut through the hot haze in her head and realize he was talking about the attack. The last thing that'd been on her mind. Mercy. How could Slade do that? With just a few kisses, he could make her forget something that had been forever branded in her memory.

He shifted again, moving her away from the crib and to a recessed area on the other side of the wall. At first she didn't know why he'd done that, but she soon figured it out. He pinned her hands to the wall and took his clever mouth to her neck.

Maya melted.

Worse, she wanted to melt. She fought to get her hands from his grip, and Slade met her gaze as if he were about to stop. But stopping was the last thing she wanted. This kiss, *this,* made her feel something she was desperate to feel. And not with just any man.

Only with Slade.

That was another red flag. She couldn't think of him that way. As a lover. But her body was in control of those thoughts now. In control of her. And the second she got her hands free from Slade's grip, she wrapped her arms around him and pulled him even closer. Until his sex was aligned with hers.

She didn't just melt. She saw stars.

"You want me to do something about this?" Slade asked, but he didn't ask permission to slide his hand beneath her top and into her bra.

He pulled back, obviously waiting, but not just waiting. He dampened his fingers with his mouth and slid all that dampness over her now exposed right nipple.

Maya heard the sound she made. Pure need. The sound of a woman ready to be dragged off to bed.

"Well?" he prompted. And he gave her left nipple the same treatment. "Let me know what you decide."

He pushed up her top, lowered his head and tongue-kissed her breasts. More fire. More ache. More everything.

"We can't," she managed to say. "Not here, not in the same room with Evan. And the door isn't locked."

He was already lowering himself to her stomach, but that stopped him, and he gave her a flat look. "That's a mixed signal."

"I know." She groaned. "It's because I really, really want you to lock that door, but Evan's here. And your family's downstairs. And we have other things we should be doing." Though she couldn't have named one other thing that didn't involve getting into bed with Slade.

It took him a moment and some mumbled profanity, but he finally eased back up, dropping a few more kisses on her breasts before he fixed her clothes. What he didn't do was move away. Slade stayed right there, his body pressed to hers and with every part of her wanting every part of him.

"I'm used to sex meaning little or nothing." He pushed her hair from her face. "I'm guessing it can't be that way with you?"

She wanted to lie, to say that she could let him satisfy this ache he'd built inside her. But Maya had to shake her head.

"That's what I thought." Slade still didn't step back. And his erection was still pressed against her, making her body rethink that head shake.

"Does that mean you'll never have sex with me?" she came right out and asked.

Now he shook his head and brushed one of those mind-blowing kisses over her mouth. "It just means I'll know beforehand that it'll be screwing things up." Another kiss. "Right now you're starting to trust me. You don't tremble when I touch you."

Maya checked. "I'm trembling now."

"Not a bad tremble." No kiss, just a deep-down gaze that seemed to slide right into her soul. "But I don't want you trembling for all the wrong reasons when I'm inside you."

That pretty much stole her breath. Mainly because she could practically feel him inside her. She could feel all the touching, the kissing and the pleasure he would give her. And Slade was right—it'd screw things up.

Still, she wanted it but clamped her teeth over her bottom lip so she wouldn't blurt it out.

It took her a moment to realize the buzzing sound wasn't in her head but that it was Slade's phone. He reached in his pocket. Not easily. Because his erection had made his jeans a very tight fit. And he extracted his phone.

"It's Declan," he said, and Slade hit the speaker button.

Just like that, the heat vanished, and she knew this call could be a warning that someone had come to the ranch looking for them.

"I hope to hell this isn't bad news," Slade growled.

"It's news. Not sure if you'll consider it good or bad." Declan paused. "I got the result from the DNA test."

## Chapter Twelve

Slade felt as if someone had punched him. Not because he'd forgotten about the DNA tests. He hadn't. But with everything else going on, it hadn't been foremost in his mind.

Even though it could change everything.

Maya sucked in her breath and held it. "Breathe," Slade reminded her. "We're listening," he said to Declan.

"This is the result on the second kidnapped baby, Caleb Rand. He's not a match to you or any of our suspects."

Maya finally let out the breath she'd been holding, but then the renewed fear flashed through her eyes. With one baby ruled out, that meant either Will Collier or Evan was likely to be Slade's son.

Fifty-fifty.

Odds that Maya no doubt hated.

"We did get a match for the baby's birth father. He's barely sixteen and spent some time in juvie lockup for an attempted B and E. Definitely not a suspect for the kidnappings. He hasn't got the money, the connections or the motive."

So the birth father hadn't given up the child and then tried to reclaim him. That really narrowed their suspects, and that meant they were back to the Colliers, Randall or Andrea.

"When will we have Evan's results?" Slade asked.

"Soon. And we might also have Will Collier's DNA."

Slade shook his head. "The estate burned to the ground. I didn't think there was any recoverable DNA."

"There wasn't in the house. But we had CSIs go through the vehicles, and they found a blanket that had fallen under the seat. They managed to get a sample, but they're not sure it's enough to run a comparison." Declan paused. "If it is, we'll compare it to yours."

"And Randall's," Slade insisted.

"Yeah. We have someone headed over to see Randall now to get a sample. And we have a court order in case he refuses."

Good. Well, it was *good* if this gave them some answers, but Slade had to consider that neither baby could be his son. Even though Deidre's doctor had said he was certain, he could have been wrong about the exact delivery date. And if that was the way the tests panned out, then his investigation was just getting started. His baby was out there somewhere. Hopefully, alive and well.

And Slade would find him.

"I'm sorry," Maya said to him the moment he ended the call with Declan.

"Thanks." He looked at her kiss-swollen mouth. Then at Evan. He could stay here with Maya in his arms, but that wouldn't do either of them much good. He had work to do, and Maya needed some rest.

"Why don't you take a nap?" And just in case she objected, he scooped her up and took her to the bed. His stupid body got an equally stupid notion that this was to continue the kissing session, so Slade made it quick. He deposited her onto the bed, gave her a chaste kiss on the cheek and headed for the door. "If you get hungry, just use the phone next to the bed, and I'll bring you up something."

"Slade?" she said just before he could leave. "Don't withhold any news from me, okay? Whether it's good or bad, I want to know."

It was a tall order because there was potentially some really bad news out there, but he nodded. And he meant it. It was hard to hold back with a woman he wanted more than his next breath.

Slade went back downstairs to find both Declan and Clayton on their phones. Stella was at the stove fixing what smelled like a pot of chili. There was corn bread baking in the oven. Dallas was seated at the table, on the phone as well, but he had his wife, Joelle, on his lap, and despite what sounded like a serious conversation about the investigation, Joelle was nuzzling his neck. Caitlyn was helping Stella but was also on the phone with her fiancé, Harlan, and it was clear from what she was saying that she missed him.

All the smells and sounds of home and all the things that usually would have sent Slade heading off to his bedroom. Even though this was his family in every sense of the word, he'd never actually felt part of it like the others. But it was good to have them all on his side because that meant they were helping Evan, too. Even if it turned out that Evan wasn't his, he wanted to do everything humanly possible to keep the baby safe.

Joelle got up from Dallas's lap and went to him. "How's Maya holding up? How are *you* holding up?" she added when their eyes met.

Since Joelle had been with him and all of his foster brothers at the Rocky Creek facility, she knew him a little better than Slade liked people knowing him. She must have seen the stress and worry all over his face. He tried to adjust his expression so it wouldn't show.

"It'll be better once we have some answers," Slade settled for saying.

Joelle gave a soft sigh, probably because he hadn't bared his heart and soul, and she kissed his cheek.

Slade frowned, not because it wasn't a nice gesture. It was. But since it was a first, Joelle must have figured things were pretty darn bad to try to comfort him with a sisterly kiss.

"Hungry?" Caitlyn asked, holding up a spoon of chili for him to sample.

But before Slade could decline, his phone rang, and he saw Randall's name on the screen.

"My P.I.s found a lead on Gina," Randall greeted. His words were rushed, and he sounded excited. "The doctor at the free clinic that Gina used decided to talk since he's worried for her safety. He admitted to delivering the baby. A boy. On September 16, the same birthday as the kidnapped babies." Randall finally paused. "That could be my son."

Yeah. And it could be the reason why these kidnappings were happening if Randall had known about the child days earlier.

"Gina used a fake ID when she had the baby, and the doctor admitted she had made plans for a private adoption. He claims he doesn't know the name of the adoptive parents."

Or maybe he wasn't saying.

Declan had already said they were sending someone over to chat with the doc, so maybe he'd spill more to the marshals than he would to P.I.s hired by the prospective birth father. Who was also a suspect in two kidnappings, two more kidnapping attempts and the murder of a hired gun who'd stolen an SUV.

"Where's Gina?" Slade asked.

"The doctor didn't know. He claims he hasn't seen her since she gave birth, and none of her friends have, either. Not that she has many friends, and they could be lying. Like Gina, her friends don't tend to be reliable."

There it was again, that jab at his ex. Ironically, Randall and he were in similar situations with an ex who'd possibly given birth to their child. And that led Slade to his next question.

"You think Gina could be dead?"

"Not a chance. I think she's laying low so I won't find her and demand to know if she stole money from me."

"Money? This is the first I'm hearing about possible stolen money."

"Because I just found out about it. My accountant was going through my books, and he found the discrepancies. If he's right, Gina might have stolen ten grand from me."

That was a good-size chunk of money, but it wouldn't go far if Gina was trying to disappear. "So you think Gina's in hiding because she stole money?"

"Why else?"

"Maybe because she's afraid of you." And Slade made sure it sounded like the accusation that it was.

Randall cursed. "So we're back to that. Look, I just want to get to the bottom of this so I can clear my name. I have no interest in Gina herself or the kid she gave up for adoption."

Which was another reason for Slade to dislike Randall. It took a special piece of slime not to care about his own child.

"I've instructed my P.I.s to keep looking for Gina for another twenty-four hours," Randall continued, "but if she hasn't turned up by then, I want this investigation to end. I'm a businessman, and something like this could hurt my reputation beyond repair."

"So would your being arrested for murder." Yeah, it was a cheap dig, but Slade was tired of this. Of this investigation. And especially tired of not having answers. He clicked the end-call button just as Declan finished his call.

"The DNA sample from Will Collier was good to go. They're already running a preliminary test, and we might have something by tomorrow."

That soon? Slade figured either way the test went, it could pose new problems, but he decided to put those on the back burner. He already had enough to deal with.

He heard the footsteps behind him and knew they belonged to Maya before he even turned around. She had Evan in her arms, and the baby was wide-awake.

"No nap, huh?" Slade went to her, took the baby

and motioned for her to sit at the table. "You need to eat something anyway."

He didn't miss the shocked looks on his brothers' faces, probably because it was the first time they'd seen him voluntarily hold a child. He'd had some cases that'd involved babies and children, but Slade had been careful to avoid being hands-on with them.

Maya was nibbling on her lip when she sat down, but Caitlyn, God bless her, came to the rescue with a smile and a bowl of chili.

Joelle smiled, too. "So what's it like to be a mom?" She patted her own stomach. "Dallas and I have one on the way."

"It's amazing," Maya said without hesitation. She didn't sample the chili until Stella, Clayton and Joelle had dished up some for everyone. "Exhausting, though. You won't get much sleep."

"After you eat, go ahead and take a nap," Slade offered. "I'll watch Evan."

Again that earned him some shocked looks, and Declan's was so bad that Slade scowled at him. The scowl was still on his face when Slade's phone rang again. Not Randall this time but another of their suspects.

"Nadine Collier," he mumbled. Since this call probably involved the investigation they were all a part of, Slade put it on speaker.

"I need your help," Nadine said the second that

Slade answered. "Look at the two pictures I'm sending you. Do it *now*."

That brought the others hurrying to his side so they could see it, as well. The photos took a while to load, and they were grainy, but he had no trouble spotting the man.

The guy was wearing a ski mask.

And he was holding something in his arms.

The second photo showed exactly what he was holding.

"He has the baby." Nadine's voice cracked. "He has us both at gunpoint."

Maya took Evan from his arms, and Slade got to his feet. "Who's holding you at gunpoint and who's the baby?"

"I don't know." It sounded as if she was crying. "On both counts. He won't let me see his or the baby's face, and he had the baby's head covered with a cap so I can't even tell the hair color. He used a stun gun on me when I was in the parking lot, and he drove me to this place. I don't know where we are, but he's holding me in a barn."

None of this could be good. Or the truth. "What does he want?"

"Money." A hoarse sob tore from Nadine's mouth.

A ransom demand. Slade had been waiting for another of those, but he hadn't expected it to come like this. "Put the man on the phone."

"He won't talk to you. I already tried. If you don't

come, if you don't help, he says he'll kill me, and no one will ever see the baby again."

Hell. This was not what Slade wanted to hear.

"You have to come," Nadine insisted. "You and Maya, and you have to bring as much cash as you can get your hands—"

"Wait a minute," Slade interrupted. "Why does he want Maya?"

"He won't say."

The color drained from Maya's face, and he probably went a little pale, too. The last place he wanted her was in the middle of a ransom exchange. It was bad enough that Nadine was there. Of course, Nadine could have orchestrated all of this, so maybe the only danger was this plan to get Maya and him out in the open.

Slade cursed. "Give your phone to our masked friend."

Nadine repeated that the man wouldn't talk to Slade, but he could hear the movement. "I got my orders," the man snarled into the phone. "If Maya Ellison doesn't come with you and if you don't have a boatload of cash, this kid is on the next flight to Mexico."

Slade tried not to react, but he wasn't immune to that threat. Even if this wasn't his baby, the infant was still in danger, and God knows what would happen to him.

"Meet me at the old Weston ranch," the man said. "You know the place?"

"Yeah." It'd been abandoned for several years, and there was only one road in and out. It was a good fifteen-minute drive from their own ranch.

"I'll go," Maya said.

"No, you won't," Slade insisted. He had to try again to bargain with the devil in the picture holding that baby. "I'll come alone." A lie. He'd have at least one of his brothers hidden away as backup. "And I can bring $20,000." They probably had that much in the safe in the ranch's office.

"Bring more," the man countered. "And don't come alone. If Maya's not with you, then the deal is off. It's the same if you bring any of your law enforcement buddies. Just Maya and you. You've got thirty minutes, or I start shooting."

"No. I need a different plan," Slade said, but he was talking to himself because the kidnapper had hung up.

## Chapter Thirteen

"You're not doing this," Slade snarled.

Maya had lost count of how many times he'd already said that, and she figured she would hear it plenty more before this was over and done.

But that wouldn't change things.

She didn't consider herself a brave person. Not with her brutal past. This had nothing to do with bravery but had everything to do with a child's survival.

"What if the kidnapper had Evan?" she tossed back at Slade. She didn't add *What if this is your child?* but she figured they were both thinking it.

"It's too dangerous." Slade finished shoving the money from the safe into a bank bag. It looked to be significantly more than $20,000, and she prayed that it'd be enough.

"It's more dangerous for the baby if I don't go."

That silenced everyone in the room. Declan, Clayton, Dallas, Caitlyn, Joelle and Stella. They were obviously all waiting for Slade to respond, but he stood there, mumbling profanity and closing the bank bag as if he might rip it to pieces at any moment.

"She's right," Declan finally spoke up. He went to the closet in the office and hauled out an equipment bag. "If it were just Nadine's life at stake, I'd never agree to this. But it's a baby, Slade."

But Slade shook his head. "A baby this kidnapper could be using as bait to draw out Maya."

"There's no reason for him to draw me out," she argued. "He could just want me there because he might think it'll keep you from firing shots at him."

"The baby would prevent me from doing that." Slade cursed again. "And maybe he's doing this to get us away from Evan so he can be kidnapped, too."

Maya pressed Evan closer to her heart to try to steady it. Her son had already spent too much time in danger, and it wasn't over.

But maybe this was the beginning of the end.

Dallas stepped forward. "You know there's no way we'd allow anyone to take Evan. You and Maya go out to the Weston ranch, and the rest of us will stay here and guard him. You can take the infrared scanner so you can see who's in that barn and anywhere else on the grounds before you go in. Harlan, Wyatt and one of the deputies can follow you and stay close in case you need backup."

"That still leaves Maya in danger." Slade's voice

was so loud that it startled Evan, and he began to cry. "Sorry," he grumbled.

"It's okay." She went closer and gave Slade's arm a gentle touch. It didn't soothe him one bit, but that was asking a lot of an arm rub.

"I can go in the truck with Maya and you," Declan volunteered. "I'll stay down so the kidnapper doesn't see me. We'll all have on Kevlar vests. And when we get there, you can go in for the money drop. If the kidnapper insists on seeing Maya, he can get a glimpse of her in the truck."

Slade was still shaking his head.

"If things don't look right, we'll get out of there fast," Declan added.

"And what if things go wrong here?" Slade asked.

Maya's breath caught in her throat. The idea of her son being in more danger was terrifying, but the danger existed no matter where he was. And this might be a way to stop it. Because if they got lucky, this wouldn't be just a money drop—they might be able to rescue the baby and capture the kidnapper.

"I'll have Sheriff Geary come out here," Dallas explained. "Plus, every ranch hand will be armed and ready."

"I can watch the baby," Stella said, stepping forward.

"I'll help," Joelle and Caitlyn offered in unison.

Maya looked down at her son. Then at Slade. She

wanted nothing more than for them all to stay put at the ranch, surrounded by his family, who would protect them at all cost. But the kidnapper had made that impossible.

"There, there," Stella whispered to Evan as she took him from Maya. She nuzzled Evan's cheek and gently rocked him. His whimpers stopped almost immediately.

"You need to put this on." Declan took several vests from the equipment bag and handed Maya one. "It's Kevlar. It'll stop a bullet."

"Yeah, but not if this SOB aims at her head." Slade snatched one of the other vests from Declan, and both Declan and he put them on.

"The kidnapper will have to go through me to get to Maya's head," Declan snarled back. "Or any other part of her, for that matter. Look, I'm not happy about this, either, but we don't have a choice."

Maya agreed, though the thought of all of them in direct danger made her sick to her stomach. At least Declan and she would be in the truck. Or that was the plan anyway. But Slade would be the one to walk inside the barn and try to negotiate the release of the baby.

"Let's go," Declan added. "I can call Harlan and Wyatt to get them headed out there."

"And I'll call Sheriff Geary and the ranch hands," Dallas volunteered.

Still, Slade didn't budge for several long moments. He finally aimed his index finger at Maya. "You'll stay down, and you won't take any chances."

It seemed as if they all made a collective sigh of relief, but there was no real relief and wouldn't be until they got the baby safely out of there.

Slade grabbed the equipment bag and some extra guns from the closet. He handed her one before they headed out. However, he paused to brush his hand over the top of Evan's head, and Maya kissed her son again.

"I'll take good care of him, I promise," Stella said. And even though Maya hardly knew this woman, she believed her.

With Declan on the phone to Harlan and Wyatt, they hurried to one of the trucks parked at the back of the house. Slade got behind the wheel, and Maya slid into the center so that Declan could take the window and keep watch. At least it was during daylight, unlike the ordeal that'd gone on at the safe house, so they'd be able to see a threat before it was too late.

Well, maybe.

"What if Nadine is behind this?" she asked. "What if she's doing this to cover up the fact that she had her adopted child kidnapped, maybe to get back at her husband? Or maybe just for the ransom?"

"If she's behind this, she'll probably have more

than one hired gun with her." Slade responded so quickly it was clear he'd already given this some thought.

However, Maya had to shake her head. "But Nadine's motive would be money to pay her gambling debts. Why demand cash from you when she could make a much larger ransom demand from her husband?"

"Because maybe that's too obvious. It'd make us key in on her even more as a suspect. This way she looks like a victim and not a perpetrator. Besides, this is just one of the babies. She could be planning to hit up Chase for a ransom for the second."

True. And maybe she hadn't asked ransom of the adopted parents of the second missing baby, Caleb, because they wouldn't have had much cash to give. Maya remembered that Slade had told her they were both schoolteachers.

Slade's attention volleyed between the side-and rearview mirrors, but he also sent one of those glances her way. "Hell," he mumbled.

That sent a jolt of alarm through her. "What?"

*"This,"* he snarled.

And when she looked into his eyes, she knew exactly what *this* meant. This attraction between them was rearing its head again and not in a heated I-want-you-now sort of way. It was creating a distraction because Slade wasn't thinking like a lawman.

"Harlan and Wyatt will get there ahead of us," Declan relayed the moment he finished his call. "They have infrared, too," he added, fishing the handheld machine from the equipment bag. "The plan is for them to move into position at the back of the barn. Deputy Randy Wells will be coming in behind us."

So there'd be five lawmen and her. Since Maya had never fired a gun, she wouldn't be much help, but she was glad she had something in case things turned bad.

"Don't you dare get shot," she mumbled to Slade.

"Same to you," he mumbled back, and he turned onto a gravel-and-dirt road.

"Fresh tracks," Declan pointed out.

The tracks didn't exactly confirm Nadine's story, but it was clear someone had recently driven out here.

With each passing second, Maya's heart beat even faster, and by the time the ranch came into view, she was fighting just to keep her breath level. It wouldn't help matters if she hyperventilated, and the last thing Slade needed was to babysit her.

"Time for you two to get down," Slade warned them. He stopped at the rust-scabbed cattle gate about two hundred yards from the house.

Maya made a sweeping glance of the house and grounds. It was nowhere near as large as Slade's family ranch, and the pasture fence was falling down in spots. The weeds and grass were at least knee-high in places, the trees and shrubs overgrown as well, and maybe that overgrowth would give Harlan, Wyatt and the deputy some cover as they made their way to the barn.

Maya got on the floor of the truck and Declan dropped down across the seat just as his phone buzzed. "Harlan," Declan greeted, but she couldn't hear the other end of the conversation.

While Declan was talking with his brother, Slade took the infrared, turned it on and aimed it at the house, then the barn. Maya levered herself up just enough to see the screen and the three colored splotches in the barn.

"He definitely has the baby," Slade commented. "And it appears to be in some kind of carrier on the floor next to the kidnapper." He tapped the other splotch. "That's probably Nadine. It looks as if her hands are tied behind her back."

That didn't mean this wasn't still a setup, but it was looking more and more as if Nadine had been telling the truth.

"Harlan and the others are coming across the back pasture now," Declan explained when he finished his call. "There's a van behind the barn, but according to infrared, no one is inside."

She didn't miss the look that passed between Slade and Declan.

"Is that bad?" she asked.

"Strange," Slade clarified. "The kidnapper must have anticipated that I'd bring in backup, so why would he come alone?"

True, and Maya could see where this was going. "Maybe he didn't come alone. Maybe Nadine isn't really tied up."

"Yeah." And that's all Slade said for several seconds before he took out his phone and redialed Nadine's number. He put the call on speaker.

But it wasn't Nadine who answered. It was the man in the barn with her. Maya could see enough of the man's movements on the screen to determine that.

"I don't see Maya with you," the man said.

Slade mumbled some profanity, squinted against the afternoon sun and pointed toward the front of the barn. *Camera,* he mouthed.

Declan mouthed some profanity, too, and fired off a text message to Harlan to warn him that there might be a camera at the rear of the building, too.

"Maya's on the seat," Slade told the man. "I don't want her in the line of fire."

"The only way I fire is if I don't see her."

The muscles in Slade's jaw stirred. "Sit up for just a second," he told her.

Maya made her way off the floor, but she barely had time to look over the dash before Slade pushed her back on the floor.

"There," Slade snarled. "You've seen her."

"Who else you got in that truck with you?" the man asked.

Maya's heart nearly stopped, but she reminded herself that the camera hadn't spotted her, so it wouldn't spot Declan. Unless the kidnapper had infrared, too.

"It's just Maya and me," Slade lied.

The kidnapper didn't say anything for several moments, but the baby started to cry. "All right, then. Now call your brothers or whoever you've got hiding in the back pasture and tell them to stop in their tracks. Do it."

Oh, God. So there'd probably been a camera back there after all. She prayed the three had gotten close enough to the barn to help if things started to unravel.

"What part of that didn't you understand?" the kidnapper taunted over the cries of the baby. "Call your backup and tell them to stop. If they move another inch forward, I shoot Mrs. Collier and hightail it out of here with the kid. Remember what I said about sending the brat to Mexico. And trust me, I don't care what kind of *family* he ends up with."

Slade mumbled some profanity, but he made the call and told his brothers and the sheriff to hold their position. "What now?" he snapped to the kidnapper.

"You drive to the barn. Stop directly in front of the door and wait until you hear from me."

"Don't let him shoot me!" she heard Nadine yell.

The woman genuinely sounded terrified, but Maya wasn't ready to trust anyone other than Slade and his family.

"Stay down," Slade repeated to her, and he did as the kidnapper had asked. He pulled the truck to a stop and waited. They didn't have to wait long. His phone rang just a few seconds later.

"Don't think about trying to take me out," the kidnapper warned, "because I got the kid in my arms. And I've put a few security measures in place to make sure you don't try to blow off my head."

*He's up and moving,* Declan mouthed.

Even though Maya couldn't see what was happening, from the sound of it, the barn door opened and the baby's cries got louder. That cut her to the core. Even though the child was too young to understand what was going on, he might be hungry or worse. God knows what kind of care this monster had given the precious baby.

"How much money did you bring?" the kidnapper asked Slade.

"At least thirty grand. It was everything we had in the safe."

The man made a sound of disapproval. "I wanted more, but I guess that'll have to do. The next kid will cost you a lot more."

Maya wasn't sure whether to be relieved or terrified that he had both babies and was willing to ransom them. Maybe this meant they'd soon recover both children. And maybe it also meant the threat to Evan was over.

"Where's the other baby?" Slade snapped.

"That's a secret." It sounded as if the guy was smiling, and Maya wished she could slap him for that. Or better yet, get Slade to beat him to a pulp. She hated this monster for putting the babies in danger.

"Just focus on getting this kid for now. We'll work out the details of the other later. Oh, and if you or your marshal brothers decide to put a bullet in me, I think you should know that'd be like putting a bullet in both kids. As you can see, I'm holding this one, and if I'm dead and gone, the other kid will just disappear."

That caused Maya's stomach to clench. This had to end. They had to recover those babies.

"Plus, there's that security measure I talked about," the man continued. "There are two assault rifles aimed at right about the spot where you've parked, and they're rigged with a sound sensor and detonators. If someone fires a shot, the assault rifles start firing, too. I'm not exactly sure where the bullets will go, and I don't think you want to find out."

Maya couldn't see the guns from her angle, but there were holes in the upper part of the barn. The guns could be positioned behind there.

"You and Maya need to step out of the truck," the kidnapper instructed. "I want the money in Maya's hands. You can keep your gun because I suspect you've got one hidden away as backup anyway. Just remember that part about bullets flying. Not a good idea."

"There's no reason for Maya to get out," Slade argued. "I can bring you the money."

"You could if that's what I'd told you to do. I didn't. I said for Maya to bring it. Or maybe you want this kid sent off to Mexico."

"I'll do it," Maya insisted. Their gazes met, and she hoped that her expression was a reminder that they had backup in place and there was no reason for the kidnapper to shoot them.

Well, no reason she could think of.

She prayed she was right about that.

Slade mumbled some profanity, and she could see the struggle going on behind those steely muscles. But there was no other option here. They couldn't risk a shootout with the baby and Nadine as hostages.

"Stay behind me," Slade insisted, and he scooped up the money bag and handed it to her. "Get out on this side."

Of course, that meant her crawling over Declan, but somehow they managed to reposition themselves so that she could exit on the driver's side behind Slade.

Maya finally got a good look at the kidnapper, who was indeed wearing a ski mask, and he had a gun in his right hand. The baby in his arms was crying nonstop now. That didn't help settle her nerves. Of course, nothing would at this point except getting the baby out of there.

Was it Morgan Gambill behind that mask?

It was possible.

He'd escaped from the sheriff's office during that fake bomb scare, and she had no doubt that he worked for the kidnapper. That slight bulge beneath the mask near his right ear also told her that he was probably wearing some kind of communicator. Maybe so the man who'd orchestrated this could give him orders.

"Is the baby Will?" Nadine called out. "I can't see his face, but I need to know if it's Will."

Maya was surprised she couldn't tell from the baby's cries. She certainly would have been able to tell if it was Evan. Of course, Nadine probably hadn't spent a lot of time with the baby she'd intended to adopt since the adoption had been Chase's idea.

"Open the money bag and drop it in front of me," the kidnapper instructed, drowning out Nadine when she repeated her question.

Even though her hands were shaking, Maya managed to open it, and Slade and she walked forward with him staying in front of her. She saw Nadine sitting on the hay-strewn floor. Her hands had been tied to a support post, and she looked as terrified as Maya felt. If this was an act, then Nadine was doing a very good job of playing the hostage victim.

"Come closer," the man ordered. They took another step just as Slade's phone rang. "Go ahead. Answer it."

That was a surprise, and Maya was instantly suspicious. Slade didn't take his eyes off the kidnapper, but he used his left hand to ease his phone from his pocket, and he handed it to Maya. She saw Declan's name on the screen and figured this wasn't good news.

"We got a problem," Declan said the moment she answered. "There are two vehicles approaching the ranch. Slade and you need to get out of there *now*."

## Chapter Fourteen

Slade couldn't hear what the caller had said to Maya, but it had her turning, and her attention zoomed to the road leading to the ranch.

"I guess that was one of your brothers letting you know we have visitors," the kidnapper calmly said.

Hell. This couldn't be good. Even though his gun was ready, Slade turned slightly so he could try to better protect Maya.

"No reason for concern," the man added. "Our visitors are just like you. They're here to bring money so you can bring this squalling kid back where he belongs."

Slade glanced at the two approaching vehicles. There was no way Declan could have seen them from his position in the truck, so that meant his brother must have used the infrared.

"Are they armed?" Slade said loud enough that Declan would hear.

Maya still had his phone pressed to her ear, and she shook her head. "He can't tell."

So that meant Declan was no doubt positioning himself in case this went from bad to worse.

"Remember, keep your fingers off those triggers," the kidnapper growled.

As if Slade needed the warning. The baby's cries were plenty enough for him to know this couldn't turn into a shooting match. Well, not unless Slade could get the baby and Maya to safety first. Then he'd like nothing more than to take this guy out.

Of course, there was the threat of the assault rifles.

It was possible to rig the rifles to fire with some kind of trigger device, but there was no way to predict the path of the bullets. That only made things more dangerous.

The two cars pulled to a stop on each side of his truck, and Slade maneuvered Maya so that she was closer to the door in case she had to run for cover and get back inside with Declan.

"It's Randall," Maya mumbled.

Yeah, it was. Randall stepped from the first car. He had a gym bag in his left hand and lifted his right hand in the air as if surrendering.

"Welcome, Mr. Martin," the kidnapper said. "Hope you brought me lots of cash."

Randall scowled at Slade and Maya as if this were somehow all their fault. "I brought what I had from my business. About $11,000." It wasn't just his expression that was hostile. His tone was, too. "Now, where the hell is Gina? And is that her kid?"

The kidnapper shook his head, and though Slade couldn't see his face, he could have sworn the guy smiled. "Sorry, no Gina."

"You bastard! You said you had her and would release her if I paid you." Randall charged forward but came to a skidding stop when the kidnapper pointed the gun at him.

"Hey, I had to say something to get you here," the kidnapper calmly answered. "And it worked. Besides, this kid *could* be hers. Trust me, I'll be more than happy to turn him over to you just as soon as I have all the money."

Randall made a sound of outrage. "I don't want the baby. I want Gina!"

"Oh, your poor thing," he mocked, but his voice took on a harder edge. "Just drop the money bag in front of me and shut the hell up."

"I want to know where Gina is," Randall fired back.

"You'll learn that *after* I have the money from all of you. Now put it on the ground and then step back by the marshal."

Slade wasn't at all sure Randall would do that, but he finally went forward. That was when Slade saw the gun tucked in the back waist of Randall's pants. He hoped to hell Randall didn't start shooting.

"He says he's got assault rifles rigged to a sensor," Slade explained to Randall. "If any of us fires, he says the rifles go off."

Randall's eyes widened, and he glanced nervously around the barn. He gave a shaky nod, dumped the bag on the ground and then went to stand beside Slade. Not the best position as far as Slade was concerned. He didn't want any of the suspects this close, but at least he could see Randall this way. The more immediate concern was the person in the other car.

"Maya, it's your turn now," the kidnapper said. "Put the money bag next to Randall's."

"Not until I know who's in the other car," Slade countered.

"I figured you'd already guessed."

Yeah, he had. "Chase Collier?"

"And the nanny, Andrea whatever-her-name-is." He made a motion with his hand, and the two stepped out. Both put their hands in the air as well, and Chase was carrying what appeared to be yet another bag of money.

Both Andrea and Chase looked terrified, normal for the situation, but there was nothing about this situation or their reactions that Slade trusted. After all, they were both suspects. As were Randall and Nadine. For all he knew, Nadine wasn't even tied up.

"Chase!" Nadine yelled. "Help me. Get me out of here."

But Chase barely spared his wife a glance. His attention went to the baby. "Is it Will?"

"We don't know, and he won't say," Slade answered.

"You can't tell from the cries?" Maya asked.

Both Andrea and Chase listened, and Andrea finally shook her head. "It doesn't sound like Will."

Then it could be the other baby, Caleb Rand. Or another baby the guy had kidnapped. It could even be Slade's child. But he forced the thought aside. The only thing that mattered now was that a baby needed to be rescued.

"How'd you know to come here?" Slade asked Randall and the others.

"I got a call from this bozo," Randall snapped. "He said he had Gina and that he was holding her hostage."

"He called me, too," Chase answered.

Andrea's attention was glued to the baby. "I was with Chase when he got the call, and I insisted on coming with him. I had to make sure Will was okay."

Later Slade would want to know why they were together, but he had bigger fish to fry—mainly getting them all out of there alive.

"Toss the money bag next to Randall's," he told Maya.

She reached around him and slung the bag in

that direction. It landed practically at the kidnapper's feet.

"And what about you, Mr. Collier?" the kidnapper asked. "How much did you bring me?"

"Fifty thousand. It'd better be enough. Now hand over the baby. And Nadine." But it certainly sounded as if he'd added his wife as an afterthought.

Nadine obviously felt the same way. Her mouth tightened to the point of looking painful.

Chase put the money next to the others, and by Slade's calculations, it was about a hundred grand. Not chump change but still not as much as the kidnapper could have gotten from a man like Chase. Of course, if the kidnapper had guessed the child might be Slade's, he could have demanded more, too. Slade himself wasn't a rich man, but since Kirby had given him and each of his brothers part ownership of the ranch, they were all doing a lot better than just okay.

So why this hasty demand?

Had something gone wrong and this guy's boss had told him to unload the baby? Or was something else going on? It was the possibility of something else that worried him most.

"You've got your money," Slade reminded the guy. "Now give us Nadine and the baby."

"I think I'll keep Nadine for a while," the man said. "But Maya can take the kid, and the rest of you can go."

Slade wasn't sure who howled the loudest—Nadine or Randall. "I'm not leaving without Gina," Randall said at the same time that Nadine yelled out, "Chase! Don't let him do this."

"You want Gina," the kidnapper said to Randall. "You need to look in Houston. A little bird told me she was in at one of those extended-stay motels called the Bluebonnet."

Randall turned and started to bolt, but Slade caught onto his arm. "Best if we all leave together," he warned Randall in a whisper. "The kidnapper could have gunmen somewhere on the road to pick us off one by one."

Randall mumbled some profanity, but he stayed put.

"Let's get the baby," Slade whispered to Maya, and he walked with her over to the kidnapper.

"No way," the guy snarled, turning his gun on Slade. "You stay put. I figure if you get hold of me, you can kick my butt six ways to Sunday. So stay back."

And the kidnapper did some moving, too. He positioned himself in front of Nadine and crouched down so that it would make it next to impossible for one of his brothers to use infrared to pinpoint the kidnapper's location and send a kill shot right at him.

That new position didn't please Slade, nor did the man's order for him to stay back, but he stopped.

"Move fast," he told Maya. "Get the baby and then get inside the truck."

Maya did exactly as he asked, and Slade knew she was moving fast, but time seemed to stop. It sent his heart crashing when he saw the kidnapper point the gun within just a few inches of Maya's head.

She wasn't faring much better.

Her hands were shaking, but she managed to take the crying baby and pulled it close to her chest as she raced toward the truck. Slade held his breath until she was inside, but he figured his breathing wouldn't return to normal until they were out of there.

"Is that Will?" Andrea called out. She rushed forward and probably would have jumped in the truck if the kidnapper hadn't pointed his gun at her.

"I don't want anybody moving. And here's what's gonna happen next. Maya, you put the baby on the seat and drive out of here. I'll keep the marshal and the others a little while longer."

"No!" Maya said, lifting her head. Nadine and Andrea shouted the same, and Nadine began to struggle even harder with the ropes.

"Yes," the kidnapper argued, his gun still aimed at Andrea. "And since I don't think anyone wants to be shot, Maya better get behind the wheel and start that engine now."

"Do it," Slade insisted when she didn't move. "Get the baby out of here," he added. Yeah, it was playing dirty. No way would she hang around an armed man and put the baby's life at risk.

Behind the kidnapper, Nadine tugged and jerked, her shoulders rocking back and forth. If the gunman noticed, he didn't say anything. He volleyed his attention in front of him, specifically at the truck.

Damn it. This could be a ruse to separate Maya from the rest of them. Was she the kidnapper's target? If so, why hadn't he tried to shoot her when she stepped from the truck?

Maybe because the kidnapper needed her alive.

But why?

Slade didn't have time to come up with an answer, because Maya started the engine and began backing out of the drive. She'd barely made it a foot when Nadine broke free of the rope. Instead of ramming her body into the kidnapper, she tried to get to her feet and run.

Not a good idea.

The kidnapper cursed, turned and latched on to her. Slade's instincts were to rush forward, to try and help Nadine, but he had an even greater need to protect Maya and the baby.

Chase and Andrea, however, both shouted and ran toward the front of the barn. Randall drew his gun. Not the best thing to steady Slade's nerves. Because now he had to watch Randall and the kidnapper.

"Try to contain the situation," Slade shouted, and he hoped his brothers could do that.

He turned so he could get into the truck. That way, if this was some kind of ruse to get Maya, both Declan and he could protect her. Besides, they needed to get the baby to the hospital ASAP just in case he'd been injured.

But the sound stopped Slade cold.

The shot blasted through the barn, and he whirled back around to see Nadine's hand on the kidnapper's gun. Judging from her horrified expression, she'd accidentally pulled the trigger in the struggle. Slade couldn't tell if she'd been shot or if she'd managed to shoot the kidnapper.

That's because a new sound snared his attention. Movement from the barn rafters, and before he could even make it to the truck, the bullets started flying.

Hell.

Since Slade knew from infrared there were no other people inside the barn, that meant the kidnapper hadn't lied about the assault rifles being rigged with a sound sensor.

Everyone dived to the ground, but Slade got into the truck. In the same motion, he pushed Maya back to the floor. Declan was still lying on the seat, the crying baby in the crook of his arm, but he handed off the baby to Maya so he could get up. He lifted his gun.

Just as some shots crashed into the front windshield. The bullet-resistant glass stopped them, but the glass cracked and webbed, making it impossible for Slade to see what was happening.

But he could hear the chaos.

Nadine was screaming nonstop. Andrea, too. But the nanny was shouting out Will's name.

"Get in the back of the truck," Slade yelled to whoever could hear him.

It wasn't ideal cover, but it was better than being out in the open. However, none of them took him up on the offer. Randall jumped to the side of his own car, and Chase and Andrea dived to the side of Chase's vehicle.

The bullets continued to smack into the truck, tearing through the metal and glass, and Slade knew he couldn't wait any longer. He had to get out of there.

He threw the truck into Reverse and slammed on the accelerator, but he had to weave around Randall's and Chase's vehicles so he could get to open space.

"Harlan and the others are closing in on the barn," Declan relayed. Declan had his phone sandwiched against his ear and his attention on the side mirrors.

Good. Maybe they could get Nadine to safety and arrest the kidnapper. They needed the man alive so he could tell them the location of the other baby.

And the name of the person who'd hired him.

Slade especially needed that so he could go after the person who'd put all these babies and Maya in danger.

The bullets continued to come at them, and once Slade was clear of the other vehicles, he turned the truck around so that the shots were going into the back rather than the windshield. The moment he was on the gravel road, he hit the accelerator again to put some distance between them and the bullets.

"Someone might try to take Maya," Slade relayed to Declan.

She gasped, but Declan only nodded. "That's why the kidnapper insisted you bring her."

"But why?" Maya asked.

That was the million-dollar question, but there was the possibility that the kidnapper wanted to use Maya to get them to turn over Evan. That wouldn't happen, but it was clear the kidnapper was desperate or he wouldn't have orchestrated this lethal situation.

"Oh, God," Maya said over the baby's cries. "What if they're at the ranch trying to take Evan?"

"We're headed there now." Slade had already considered this possibility, and even though the ranch was well protected, he didn't want Maya on the road any longer than necessary. Once he had gotten her and the baby to safety, he could call the hospital and arrange for a doctor to check out the baby.

And figure out who the child was.

Slade was hoping it was either Will or Caleb because he didn't want any other kidnapped babies added to this.

Declan's phone buzzed, and he answered the call while he kept watch.

"Harlan says they made it into the barn," Declan relayed. But then he paused, cursed. "And it's not good. They found a dead body."

## Chapter Fifteen

The only thing Maya could do was wait and try to soothe the crying baby. His sobs tapered off to whimpers, but there was no tapering off of the emotion on Declan's and Slade's faces.

Declan stayed on the phone just listening to whatever Harlan was telling him, and whatever it was, it wasn't good.

*They found a dead body.*

If that body belonged to the kidnapper, then they might have lost their main lead to the other missing child.

Perhaps Slade's son.

Of course, the alternative wasn't much better—that Randall, Chase, Nadine or Andrea was dead. Maya wasn't especially fond of any of them, but if one of them happened to be the person behind the kidnapping, then the missing baby might be lost forever.

Mumbling profanity, Declan ended the call and

looked over at Slade. "Andrea is dead. And the kidnapper got away with the money."

Oh, mercy. Definitely not good news, and worse—if the kidnapper escaped, did that mean he was on the road behind them? It seemed a selfish thing, considering that a woman was dead, but if the man started shooting again, the baby could be hurt.

"Where's the kidnapper?" Maya managed to ask despite the fact her lip was trembling.

"He got in the van and drove across the pasture. There's probably an old ranch trail back there. But Harlan's in pursuit while Wyatt and the deputy stay with the Colliers and Randall."

Yes, because if the kidnapper returned, one of them could be shot, as well. Of course, that meant Harlan was headed right into the line of fire by trying to chase down this guy.

It seemed to take Slade several moments to get his jaw unclenched. "How'd all of this happen?"

Declan shook his head and continued his watch of their surroundings. "By the time Harlan and the others got to the barn, they found Andrea dead by the side of Chase's car. A single gunshot wound to the head."

The last time Maya had seen Andrea, the woman had been running for cover. With all those bullets flying, though, there'd been no safe place to hide. "What about the others? Were they hurt?"

Declan shook his head again. "Nadine's screaming at Chase for not doing more to save her, and Randall's riled that Wyatt won't let him leave so he can go to Houston to look for his ex-girlfriend. Chase is demanding that he see the baby we have so he'll know if it's Will."

It shouldn't have surprised her that none of them had asked about the child's condition. Or if he was safe. At least Chase was asking something about the baby, but that could all be for show. To make himself look innocent. The truth was he had just as strong of a motive as the others if he was trying to frame Nadine so that he wouldn't have to split his vast estate with her.

"I'll call Dallas and get him to send me a photo of both babies," Declan offered.

Maya looked up at Slade at the exact moment he looked down at her. "I'm sorry. I don't want to know how many bad memories that brought back for you, but I figure it was *bad*."

She saw the worry and guilt practically weighing him down. Not for himself but for her. It was touching, and unnecessary.

"We got out with the baby," she reminded him, and looked down at the little boy. He'd fallen asleep, probably exhausted from all the crying, but with his face relaxed she was able to look at it and compare it to Slade's. She didn't see any resemblance, but then, it was hard to tell with babies.

And the truth was, he looked more like Evan than this baby.

That was a bitter pill to swallow in some ways, but in others, sharing custody with Slade suddenly didn't seem so bad.

If he shared, that is.

Maybe it was the fact they'd come so close to dying again, but she didn't believe he would just take Evan from her. No. Slade cared. She cared for him, too. But it was worse than that.

She was falling in love with him.

Not exactly the best time for that to hit her, but there was no good timing for this.

"We're on the ranch grounds," Declan told her, and he helped her onto the seat with the baby just as the photos of the two missing children appeared on his phone.

Maya looked at both, then eased off the baby's knit cap so she could compare him to the shots. "This is Caleb Rand," Declan and she said at once.

There was no mistaking it. Of course, the photo was probably only a few days old since the adoptive parents likely would have taken many pictures of the child. Well, they would have if they were better parents than the Colliers.

Declan called Dallas and relayed the info so that Dallas could call the child's adoptive parents. It was a relief to know the child's identity, but there it was again. The questions in Slade's eyes.

If this wasn't his child, then where was he?

Slade pulled to a stop in front of the ranch house, and they all hurried up the steps. Slade's family was there waiting for them, and even though the baby was sound asleep, Stella hurried across the foyer to bring her Evan. Caitlyn took the other baby so that Maya could take Evan.

Maya instantly felt her heart rate decrease, and even though it wasn't, it was as if she'd stepped into her home.

She was clearly losing it.

This wasn't her home, but holding Evan put everything in perspective. He was safe, thanks to Slade and his family, and for now she pushed all her other worries aside. Well, she managed it until Dallas finished the phone call he was making and gave his brothers a glance she'd come to know all too well.

He had bad news.

"Harlan lost the kidnapper," Dallas said.

There was a collective groan in the foyer. Without the kidnapper, they didn't have a lead on the other baby, and that meant the danger would continue.

"Wyatt and the others will get statements from Chase, Nadine and Randall," Dallas went on. "They'll take a look at their phones to see what time they got the ransom calls. And there's a CSI crew on the way to the barn to collect any possible evidence."

She could only hope and pray that the kidnapper had left something incriminating behind.

"What about the baby's adoptive parents?" Slade asked. Because he was looking down at Evan, Maya moved closer and eased him into Slade's arms.

Yet something else that felt like home.

"The Rands are on the way here," Dallas answered. "Needless to say, they're very happy about their son being rescued. I told them the doc would have to check him out first, and they agreed." He glanced at his watch. "Dr. Landry should be here within the next half hour."

"How is Mrs. Rand? I remember Slade said the kidnapper clubbed her when he took the baby."

"She's out of the hospital and well enough to travel."

That was something at least. Of course, even a serious injury probably wouldn't have stopped the woman. It wouldn't have stopped Maya.

Caitlyn looked down at the sleeping baby she was holding. "Should I change his diaper or something?"

"Not yet." Slade glanced at Declan. "Want to check the baby for any signs of...anything?"

Because of the fatigue, it took a moment for that to sink in, and then her heart went to the floor. Caitlyn had a similar reaction because the color drained from her face, and she hurried into the living room and eased down on the sofa. They all followed her, and Maya worked herself to the front of them.

She prayed the monster hadn't hurt this child.

Caitlyn turned back the blanket and then lifted the baby's loose blue top and tugged off the stretchy bottom. There wasn't a mark on him, and the relief caused Maya to wobble. Since Slade's hands were occupied with Evan, it was Stella who caught onto her.

"See," Stella said in a soft, comforting whisper, "the little guy's just fine."

"We'll need his clothes and diaper bagged," Dallas insisted. "Especially that diaper. It's easy to leave fingerprints on the adhesive tapes."

That reminder sent them scattering. Dallas said something about getting an evidence bag from his truck. Joelle hurried to the kitchen to grab a fresh diaper from the supplies they'd gotten for Evan. There were extra clothes in that bag, too, and a blanket.

Stella gave Maya's arm a nudge. "You look ready to fall on the floor. A hot bath will help. Some rest, too. And Joelle brought over some clothes and put them in your room. You two are about the same size."

Maya shook her head. "I don't want to leave Evan." Or Slade.

"They'll be just fine," Stella said as if she knew exactly what Maya was thinking. "And if we hear anything about the kidnapper or the case, Slade can come up and tell you all about it."

"She's right." Slade walked closer. "Get some rest, because it could turn out to be a long night. We'll have to make our official statements about what went on in that barn."

Mercy, she'd forgotten all about the administrative mop-up that'd have to be done. With Andrea's death, this was now a murder investigation, and there was still one baby missing.

"I'll have some food brought up in an hour or so," Slade added, and he kissed her cheek. Pulled back. Stared at her. And then kissed her for real.

Just like that, her brain went hazy again, and it wasn't from the adrenaline crash. One kiss from Slade could make her forget all about the fear, danger and uncertainty.

Potent stuff.

And the kisses played with her breath. She couldn't seem to catch it, and when Slade pulled back, his eyebrow lifted.

"Rest," he insisted. His voice was a whisper now. "Better go now before I change my mind about what you should be doing."

She bit back a laugh and then remembered they weren't the only two people in the room. Somehow she'd managed to forget that. But thankfully the others were all caught up in the things that needed to be done for the Rand baby and the investigation. Well, all but Stella, and she was trying not to smile.

Maya gave Evan a kiss and headed up the stairs

to the guest room. Her legs got more tired with each step, and by the time she reached the guest room, she wasn't even sure she could make it to the shower. However, she forced herself in there anyway. She stripped down, leaving a trail of clothes, and made her way into the steamy water.

Instant relief.

Well, sort of.

The heat relaxed her muscles anyway, but Slade's kiss was still causing her body to ache for other things.

Especially *him*.

Sex would complicate things. Would blur lines best left clear and untouched, but still she ached. It'd been so long since she'd felt anything like this. And never had the ache been this strong and relentless. It was as if she needed him, and that worried her more than the ache.

When she finished her shower, Maya found the stack of clothes that Joelle had sent her. There was a gown, cotton and a little on the thin side. Since that would only make Maya think of Slade removing the gown, she went with a pair of jeans and a top. She dressed, made her way back into the bedroom and cursed when she felt the disappointment.

Slade wasn't there.

So much for her insane fantasies of having him instead of a much-needed nap.

Maya dropped down on the bed and tried to sleep.

She failed but tossed and turned while the bad part of herself wished Slade would appear at her door. She was so caught up in the fantasy of that happening that she gasped when there was a real, soft knock.

A moment later the door opened, and Slade peeked in. "Figured you'd have trouble sleeping, so I brought you something to eat."

He had a tray with a sandwich and what smelled like chicken soup. It was probably delicious and she was hungry. But Maya stood and found herself going for Slade instead of the tray.

He stepped in, closed the door and set the tray on the dresser. "Stella says she'll watch Evan for the night so we can get some rest."

Okay, that brought her back from fantasyland. She hadn't forgotten about Evan, but Stella's offer was a reminder that her son would want to be fed soon, and he'd need to be bathed.

"Her offer's not lip service," Slade added. "Stella loves kids and wants to do this."

Yes, but it was something Maya should be doing. Something she *wanted* to do. And she would.

Soon.

But for now she accepted Stella's offer of some time, and Maya knew exactly what she wanted to do with that time.

Before she could change her mind or remember all the reasons why this was a bad idea, she slid her hand around the back of Slade's neck. Pulled him down to her.

And kissed him.

THE KISS DIDN'T surprise Slade. He'd seen it coming. Hell, it'd been coming since the first time they'd laid eyes on each other. But he wasn't sure he was ready for the timing of this. Clearly, Maya had other ideas.

Nothing about this was right, but it didn't feel wrong. He should be backing away. Should give Maya a chance to catch her breath or think.

But Slade didn't want her thinking.

He wanted her in his arms like this. Wanted that needful look in her eyes. Wanted the taste of her in his mouth.

He got all of those things.

And more.

She kissed him as if she had no doubts. But she had plenty of them, all right. It was just the fire that was drowning them out. The doubts would return, he knew that, and that should have stopped him, too.

It didn't.

He was certain the only thing that would stop him now was Maya saying no. Judging from the heat of the kiss, no wasn't going to come from her lips. So he just went with it and returned the kiss.

Man, did he.

The other times he'd kissed her, he'd tried to hold back. She hadn't needed a full dose of a man she likely feared. But along with the doubts, the fear wasn't there, either.

"Can you take this off?" She ran her hand over his holster and broke the kiss only long enough to ask the question.

Slade kept kissing her when he removed it and dropped it onto the dresser next to her tray of food. He cursed the rough way he pushed her against the wall. The need was burning him to ash, too, and he tried to stave it off with some deep kisses. It worked.

For a little while anyway.

Then the kisses just fueled the fire even more, and they fought to get closer to each other. They succeeded. Her breasts landed against his chest. Her sex against his.

That wasn't enough, either.

Slade shoved up her top, pulled down her bra and kissed her breasts. Despite the hot haze in his head, he listened for any sound of hesitation, but the only sounds she was making were those little moans of need.

Maya surprised him when she caught onto his shoulders, turned him and reversed their positions. His back landed against the wall, and she yanked up his shirt. Not just up but over his head, and she sent it sailing across the room.

"Yes," she said, and her warm, damp breath hit against his chest when she kissed him there. Then, lower. She dropped some kisses on his stomach.

Mercy. It was the purest form of torture.

And it wasn't torture that he'd allow to continue if he wanted this to last long enough to satisfy a few fantasies of his own. Of course, satisfying those with Maya would take more than a time or two.

A truly unsettling thought.

He wasn't the type for long, messy affairs, and he was certain of two things right now. Maya and he would have sex, and it would make their lives messier than they already were.

That still didn't stop him.

Nope.

With her wrapped in his arms, Slade scooped her up and went to the bed. He dropped her onto the mattress a little harder than he'd intended, but suddenly speed seemed to matter. Maya went after his clothes as if this had to happen now.

It sure felt as if it did.

Slade went after her clothes, too, and stripped off first her top, then the jeans. Even in the frenzy, their gazes met. And Maya froze.

"My scars," she said on a rise of breath.

He gave her a few seconds to scramble away and cover herself. Not that it was what he wanted her to do. Nope. He wanted her naked, but he also knew this was the first time she'd been with a man since her attack, and he didn't want to add to the nightmare she already carried with her.

Her eyes stayed wide.

Her breath frozen.

"They're just scars," he reminded her. "And they mean you're not just alive, you're a survivor."

Slade lowered his head and kissed her. Slow and gentle. First her mouth. Then her neck. Her breasts. And the scars.

One by one.

He lingered a bit on the one on her lower stomach, and he kept kissing her there until her breath returned. The soft moans, too, and she slid her fingers into his hair. Not pushing him away.

But urging him closer.

Slade obeyed.

He slid off her panties and moved the kiss even lower to the center of all that heat and need. Within just a few seconds, he could feel her so close to release, and that's how Slade intended to finish her off.

Maya had other ideas.

With her hand still gripped in his hair, she dragged him back up her body until he was on top of her. Again, she froze for just a split second. Maybe she was having flashbacks. But if so, they quickly disappeared, because she kissed him and maneuvered herself so she could help shove off his boots and jeans.

Before his jeans landed on the floor, Slade fumbled in his pocket so he could locate his wallet. "Condom," he growled.

Somehow he managed to get the darn thing on. No thanks to Maya.

Again he tried to go with the gentle approach when he entered her. Again he failed. And Slade just gave up and let Maya's frantic moves set the pace. His own pace soon became frantic, too, and the need for her took over every single thought in his head.

He moved inside her. Faster. Harder. Deeper. Until everything pinpointed to finishing this. The climax hit her, racking her body, but in that moment, with her eyes glazed with passion and her face flush with arousal, her gaze met his.

*Slade,* she mouthed.

That was it. All that he needed to send him right over the edge. Slade buried his face against her neck and did something he rarely let himself do.

He surrendered.

*Chapter Sixteen*

Wow.

Maya had expected for sex with Slade to be amazing, but she hadn't expected it to be something well beyond that. Nor had she expected for her mind to be so clear. No flashbacks of the attack. Just the dreamy feel of pleasure sliding through her entire body.

"You're better than years of therapy," she mumbled.

Slade lifted his head, the corner of his mouth lifting, too, and he eased off her and headed to the bathroom. Instant loss of his body heat and weight. She missed both, and even though the room wasn't exactly chilly, she definitely felt cold, and climbed under the covers.

The thoughts came.

Of course they did.

She had no experience in handling sex with a man she hardly knew. But she rethought that. Timewise she hardly knew Slade, but it was weird. It was as if she'd known him her entire life. She was too grounded in reality—boy, was she—to believe something this strong could happen this fast, but that didn't stop the *l* word from going through her mind.

It was probably on Slade's mind, too.

And not in a good way.

He was no doubt ready to panic right now because he'd be worried that she would see this as some kind of commitment. After all, it'd been years since she'd had sex, and she'd fallen straight into bed with him.

Slade came back into the room, and Maya opened her mouth to tell him that this was a no-commitment kind of sex, but her jaw dropped when she saw him naked. Her mouth went dry. And just like that, she was ready for sex again.

Whatever was better than drop-dead hot, Slade was it.

"This means nothing," she blurted out. Which wasn't at all the way she wanted to word that. "The sex, I mean." His aroused body certainly seemed to mean *something.*

He climbed under the covers with her, pulled her close. "I'm guessing that's your way of giving me an out."

Slade had a way of cutting right to the bottom line, and Maya nodded.

"You want me to give you an out, too?" he asked.

She blinked. Clearly, it was going to be impossible to hide her feelings and insecurities. "I'm not sure."

"Then why don't we let this just be about sex. The next time can be about something else."

Maya didn't think. She just opened her mouth and the words sort of flew out. "There'll be a next time?"

He lifted his head. Gave her a flat look. "What do you think?"

"I think there'll be a next time."

Slade made a sound of agreement and kissed the top of her head.

Even though they could both use a nap, Maya couldn't make her mind rest. The thoughts just kept flying through her head. The worries, too. Slade really didn't know what he was getting into with her and his promises of "next time."

"The condom wasn't necessary." More blurting out. "I can't get pregnant, and it's been ages since I've had sex. I figure you're tested for anything we could have passed on to each other."

"Tested, yeah. But I've never had sex without a condom, so there's nothing to pass on."

"Never?"

He looked at her again. "Fatherhood scared the hell out of me. I even used a condom with Deidre, but I guess something went wrong." He pulled her back into his arms. "I'm sorry you can't get pregnant."

She almost dismissed it, but it wouldn't do any good. Slade knew when she was lying. "It still hurts. Having Evan helps a lot, though." She winced. "Sorry, I didn't mean that to sound as if I'm asking you to back off. If he's your son…"

What?

It was too painful for Maya to think of losing her baby.

"If he's mine," Slade said, "we'll work it out."

She was about to press, to ask him exactly what he meant by that, but his phone rang. Slade cursed, rolled away from her and without leaving the bed, he located it.

"It's Clayton," he said, glancing at the screen.

Maya groaned. She'd yet to get a call with good news from his brothers, so she braced herself for another nightmare to start. She got up and started gathering her clothes.

"Is Lenora okay?" Slade asked.

That stopped Maya in her tracks, and even though she was naked, she turned back around to face him. If it was bad news, it sure didn't show on Slade's face.

"Call me when you can." Slade hung up, and the corner of his mouth lifted. "Lenora's water broke. Clayton's taking her to the hospital now."

It took a moment for it to sink in that this wasn't just good news, it was wonderful. A baby was about to be born.

"I'll go downstairs and see if anything needs to be done." Slade started dressing. "Clayton was working on certain parts of the investigation, and I can finish that up for him."

"I can help, too."

Slade shook his head. "Help by getting some rest."

Rest was no doubt impossible anyway, and she was about to tell him that when his phone rang again. Maya glanced at the clock. It'd been less than a minute since Clayton's call, and she prayed nothing had gone wrong on the drive to the hospital. She dressed even faster than she'd planned in case Slade had to leave.

"Hell," Slade said when he glanced at the phone screen. "Blocked number." He pushed the button to answer and put it on speaker.

"Marshal Becker?" the caller said.

With just those two words, Maya's heart slammed against her chest. Because it was a voice she recognized. It was the masked kidnapper who'd gotten away.

Slade grabbed a notepad from the nightstand and scribbled something for her to read: "Call Declan." He tipped his head to the house phone and wrote down Declan's number.

Maya didn't waste any time doing that, but as she dialed the number, she hurried to the other side of the room so the kidnapper wouldn't hear what she was doing.

"The kidnapper's on the phone with Slade," she whispered to Declan.

"I'll be right there," Declan assured her, and Maya quickly finished getting dressed, then ran to open the door.

"You listening, Marshal?" the kidnapper asked.

"Yeah. What do you want?"

"Well, for one thing I'd like to get rid of this other kid. You up for another ransom payment?"

Oh, God. Not another one.

Slade's jaw turned to iron. "That didn't work out so well last time. A woman's dead."

"Not by my hand."

"Then whose?"

"Not really sure, but I'm in this for the money only. Let me make this easy for you. I did some checking, and Maya and you have got some money. Your brothers, too. I'm thinking with just a phone call to the bank, you can have a quarter of a million within the next hour. And that's exactly how long I'm giving you to get out here with the cash."

With his gun drawn and his breath gusting, Declan came rushing into the room and no doubt heard that last part. He spared Slade a glance, slapped off the light switch and hurried to the window.

"We got a problem," Declan mumbled.

Yes, and the problem was on the phone with Slade. But something else had gotten Declan's attention.

Slade looked at his brother, cursed and returned to his call. "Where the hell are you?" he demanded.

"Oh, didn't I mention that? I'm at the ranch. Not the abandoned one. Your family's ranch. I'll call you with further instructions." And he hung up.

"EVAN," MAYA SAID. She would have raced out of the room if Slade hadn't caught onto her.

"Wait here, just a minute or two." Slade shoved his phone into his pocket and grabbed his holster and gun. "Where is this SOB?" He hurried to the window next to Declan and looked out.

"On the way up the stairs, I got a call from Cutter. He said someone broke through the back fence on the west side of the property. It tripped a security sensor, and he's headed back there now to check it out."

Hell. He didn't want Cutter, their head ranch hand, getting shot, and that's exactly what would happen if he hurried out there. "Call Cutter. Tell him to come back to the house so we can regroup."

Slade tried to give Maya a reassuring look, but he was certain he failed. She'd heard every word of his conversation with the kidnapper and knew what they were about to face. The trick was to face it while keeping everyone safe.

Slade looked down at the flurry of activity that was going on around the ranch. There was an ambulance and a car he didn't recognize. The sheriff's truck was there, too.

And he heard the footsteps on the stairs.

A moment later, Stella appeared in the doorway, and she had Evan in her arms. Maya ran to her and took the baby.

"I didn't know where I should go," Stella said. "Cutter called and said for us to all stay away from the windows, that we might have an intruder."

"We do." Slade wished he could temper that with a maybe, but the call from the kidnapper had come just at the time of the security alarm. He figured that wasn't a coincidence.

"So we need to get ready for the worst," Stella mumbled. "What should I tell the others? Dr. Landry's here. She came in an ambulance in case they had to take the baby to the hospital in a hurry. And the baby's adoptive parents just arrived, too."

Slade didn't want to have to deal with anyone other than the kidnapper, but it might not be safe for his family or the others to be on the grounds. "Tell everyone to stay put and away from the windows. Turn off all the lights, too."

Stella gave a shaky nod and headed back out of the room. Maya hugged Evan and climbed on the bed with him. The baby was sleeping, thank goodness, and maybe he'd stay that way. While he was hoping, he added that maybe this would all turn out to be a hoax.

"Cutter's on the way back," Declan relayed the moment he finished his call. "Should I call the bank and ask them to bring out money ASAP?"

"Yeah." Slade didn't even have to think about that. This guy wanted cash, and Slade wasn't about to risk a baby's life for money.

If there was a baby.

Unlike last time, Slade had no photo. When the kidnapper called back, he would demand proof before he met this moron face-to-face.

His phone rang, and Slade expected to see the blocked number, but this time it was a familiar one. Randall.

"I just got a call from the kidnapper," Randall said the moment Slade answered. "I thought you marshals had arrested him by now."

"He got away. Why'd he call you?" Though Slade could certainly guess.

"Same as before. He wants money, and he's giving me an hour to get it. I'm trying to find Gina, and I don't have time for another game of ransom and rescue."

Slade hated this weasel's attitude, but Slade was just as sick of these dangerous antics as Randall. "Did he tell you who this child is?"

"Didn't tell me anything other than to show up at your place with more money."

"Do it," Slade ordered. "Get out here as fast as you can. Not inside the house. Wait in the driveway." There were already too many people to keep track of, and he didn't want one of their suspects in the house.

And speaking of suspects, Slade ended the call with Randall and phoned the Colliers.

Chase answered on the first ring. "I can't talk now, Marshal."

"Yeah, I know. You got another ransom demand. I got one, too."

"Well, pay it. This has to be Will. He's the only other missing baby."

The only missing baby they knew of. There could be others, but Slade wasn't about to dash Chase's hopes. Well, if that was indeed hope. It was still possible that all of this had been a ruse to get Nadine arrested, and if Chase was behind it, he was also racking up a tidy sum of money.

Of course, the same could be said of Nadine.

"Where's your wife?" Slade asked.

"On the way to the bank to get the money. She was already in town at the hospital getting checked out. Not that was she hurt, but she insisted. So I called the bank manager and authorized her to draw a half million from my account."

"You trust her to do that?"

"I had no choice." Chase cursed, and they were pretty strong words. "I needed to arrange some security. After what happened to Andrea, I'm not taking any chances, and I want a bodyguard with me."

Slade hated to mention the obvious, but... "What if Nadine runs with the money?"

"Then I'll have the pleasure of having her butt arrested, and then I can negotiate a deal with the kidnapper."

Maybe not an easy thing to do, but Slade didn't get a chance to voice that. He got another call, and he saw the blocked number on the screen again.

"Gotta go," he told Chase, and he switched over to the other call. The first thing he heard was a baby crying. Since he'd put the call on speaker, Maya heard it, too, and she sucked in her breath.

"I want a photo," Slade insisted. "Because as far as I know, that could be a recording."

"No recording," the man snarled. "This is the real deal. He's crying his head off, is probably hungry and doesn't like being with me very much."

Slade wished he could reach through the phone and beat some sense into this man, but he held on to his temper. "A photo," he repeated.

"Yeah, yeah. Hold on to your shorts a sec." There were some clicking sounds. "Not his best angle probably, but you can see that it's a living, breathing kid. For now."

Slade clenched his phone so hard that he was surprised it didn't crush in his hand, and he watched the photo load. Definitely a baby in a carrier next to a ski-mask-wearing man. This baby was also wrapped in a thick blanket and had a cap on his head.

"Satisfied?" the man asked over the baby's cries, but he didn't wait for Slade to answer. "Here's how it'll work this time. Just as soon as the others get there with the money, you and Maya come out to the back west pasture. On horseback. Don't bring the others, just the money."

Slade was shaking his head before the guy finished. "No. I don't want Maya out there. Not after what happened to Andrea."

"As I said, that wasn't me. And it'll be different this time. Less people around. You two will drop off the money, and I'll hand you the kid. Of course, the rule is you gotta come alone. That means no brothers within sniper distance. Because I got a sniper or two of my own, and you wouldn't want the brat caught in the cross fire, would you?"

"I don't want anyone caught in the cross fire," Slade verified. "Especially Maya. That's why I and I alone will bring the money out to you."

"No deal. Maya's my insurance policy. I know as long as she's with you, you won't be planning some kind of attack. Say, I'm thinking this is more than just a protective-custody kind of thing between you two. Am I right?"

"None of your damn business," Slade snapped. "And Maya's not going out there with you."

"Then you got a problem, Marshal. Because without her, you don't get the kid. And this is a special kid you'll definitely want to get. Wanna know why?"

A chill went through Slade. Like blades of ice. "Why?"

"Because this kid is *yours*."

*Chapter Seventeen*

Maya scrambled off the bed and got to Slade as fast as she could. Every muscle in his body had gone stiff, and he stood there staring at the phone.

"Impossible. What makes you think I even have a kid?" Slade asked the caller. "The baby couldn't be mine."

At first Maya couldn't figure out why he'd lied, but then she realized this could all be a bluff or fishing expedition, and Slade didn't want to give this monster any more ammunition to use against them.

He already had plenty enough.

"Not impossible," the kidnapper fired back. "And once you test his DNA, you'll know."

If this was Will, then the DNA test was already in the works, but that didn't mean the kidnapper had run a test, too.

"You're taking a lot of risks," Slade said to the kidnapper. "You're sure this is just about the money?"

"What else would it be about? And yeah, it's

risky. A pain, too, to get three *daddies* to cough up cash at the same time. But hey, this is enough cash to make it worth all the risks." Slade shook his head as if trying to clear it. "I don't want Maya in on this," he repeated.

"Tough. You've got your orders—now follow them. Oh, and I gotta say, this kid looks just like you."

And he hung up.

Slade groaned, scrubbed his hand over his face and looked again at the photo the kidnapper had sent him. It was hard to see the baby's features, and since he was wearing a hat, Maya couldn't tell his hair color.

She touched Slade's arm and rubbed gently. "I don't want to be out there, either, but we don't have a choice."

"I'll find a choice." He cursed and moved away from her. Back to the window.

"What do you want me to do?" Declan asked.

Slade didn't answer. He stood there staring out, with no doubt an avalanche of emotions crushing him.

"We can do this like before," Maya offered. "We'll wear those bulletproof vests—"

"No," Slade mumbled.

Maya huffed, laid a sleeping Evan on the bed and went back to Slade. "I won't let you trade me for your son."

"We don't even know if it is my son. I don't intend to trust a kidnapper."

"He has a baby, Slade. We saw his photo. If it's not your son, it's Will Collier. Either way, we have to do this."

"Maya's right," Declan said, earning a glare from Slade.

But his glare faded, and his groan turned to profanity. He didn't want to do this, but he would. Because it didn't matter whose child was out there; Slade would need to save him. It only made her care for him more.

If that was possible.

"We can't rule out the possibility that this is a trap to get us out of the house," Slade finally said to his brother. "So you, Wyatt, Maya and I will ride out with the money when it arrives. Wyatt and you will hang back, and we'll position some of the ranch hands with rifles on the barns."

"Sheriff Geary's here," Declan reminded him.

"I want him, Dallas and Harlan to stay inside with Evan just in case something goes wrong."

Maya appreciated the protection for Evan and the others even though she wasn't sure the kidnapper still wanted to get to her son. The plan seemed to have changed with Caleb's release. Maybe this was solely about money now, which could point the finger at Nadine. Of course, it didn't eliminate Chase or Randall. Chase could still be trying to set up Nadine, and Randall could be doing this to locate his ex.

In other words, they weren't any closer to learning who was behind this.

However, if they recovered this last missing baby, that was a start. Maya's stomach clenched, though. Without learning the identity of the person behind this, she would always be looking over her shoulder. Always worrying if someone might try to take Evan from her. It seemed too much considering that Slade might have a claim on him, as well.

The phone calls and the planning began. Slade used the house phone next to the bed, and Declan called the ranch hand Cutter so he could alert the other hands as to what was going on. Maya went back to the bed and held her son. Even though he was asleep and had no idea of the danger, it soothed her raw nerves just to have him in her arms.

Time seemed to crawl by, and with each passing second, the fear and doubts came. That wouldn't change anything, and it certainly wouldn't stop her. Slade had put his life on the line several times for her son, and she'd do the same for this baby. Even if it turned out not to be his.

But what if it was?

Slade would have no hold on Evan. And that meant he had no hold on her.

Well, not a legal one anyway.

Her heart had already taken the leap in his direction, but she had no idea if Slade felt the same about her. If he didn't, if this was a walk-away situation between them, then this baby could mean that she'd never see him again.

A truly heartbreaking thought.

She heard footsteps again, and while there'd been no indication that anyone had broken into the house, both Declan and Slade drew their guns. That didn't help the knot in her stomach, but the person who appeared in the doorway was Dallas. He had an equipment bag that he placed on the floor, but not before he glanced at the rumpled covers on the bed and then looked at Slade and her.

Dallas had no doubt figured out what had gone on here, but thankfully he didn't mention it. Neither did Declan when Dallas and he looked at each other.

There were more footsteps, and Stella came into the room. "I can take Evan to the family room so you can get ready. The Rands are down there. Caitlyn and Joelle, too. We'll take good care of him."

That went without saying, but Maya appreciated it anyway. She handed Evan over to Stella and was surprised and warmed when the woman kissed her on the cheek.

"It'll be okay," Stella whispered. "Kirby's boys know what they're doing."

They did, but Maya knew things could go wrong. Maya gave her son a kiss and felt that fist around her heart when Stella walked out with him. Dallas and Declan left, no doubt to get started on the plan they'd come up with to keep everyone safe. Maya busied herself by putting on the Kevlar vest and barely had it on when Slade's phone rang again.

"Company's almost there." The kidnapper's voice poured through the room as soon as Slade put the call on speaker. "I got somebody watching the road, and both the Colliers and Randall will pull up in front of your house in the next couple of minutes. But there's been a change of plans."

Slade cursed. "The only change better be that Maya can stay here."

"Sorry, no can do. But you'll have a little company on the ride out to the pasture. I want you to bring Randall and the Colliers with you."

Mercy. She didn't want those people near her. Or the baby.

"Why the hell would you want those vipers to come?" Slade asked.

"More insurance. You saw what happened the last time when bullets started flying. A woman was killed. Well, I got the same guns rigged, and I figure the more targets, the less likely you or your brothers will take aim at me."

The same setup as last time. Maya could only pray the results would be different. She only wanted the baby and didn't want anyone else dying.

"By the way, did you run any tests on that bullet that killed the nanny?" the kidnapper tossed out there.

"It's in the works, but why don't you tell me what those results will be?" Slade demanded.

The man made a sound of smug amusement. "From my angle, it sure looked like Nadine pulled the trigger."

"Why would she do that?"

"Oh, come on, Marshal. You didn't see the way Chase was drooling all over Andrea? It's my guess they were playing beneath the sheets, and Nadine took the opportunity to do away with her competition."

That might be a solid theory if Nadine loved her husband. She clearly didn't. But that didn't mean Nadine would tolerate having another woman in the picture. Nadine didn't seem to be the sharing type.

"When you do the tests on the bullet, compare them to the gun that Nadine wrestled away from me."

"You mean the gun you let her wrestle away," Slade countered.

"That's good, Marshal." More of that gloating taunt. "That could have happened. Or not. I'll tell you what. When this is over and you have the kid and I'm on my way out of the country, why don't you ask her all about that?"

"Trust me, I will."

"Randall and the Colliers are here," Declan relayed from the window.

"Showtime," the kidnapper announced. "You've got fifteen minutes to get everyone and the money out here, or I'm leaving with the baby."

The man made another of those gleeful sounds that sickened Maya. "Didn't I tell you that I have another party interested in buying this kid? Take the call off speaker, Marshal, and I'll tell you all about it. Wouldn't want the details to upset Maya. Women get funny about this kind of thing."

Slade stared at the phone, and for a second Maya thought he wouldn't do it, but he finally clicked the button to end the speaker function, and he brought the phone to his ear.

Maya moved closer, but she couldn't hear what the kidnapper was saying. However, she did see the effect it had on Slade. He cursed and pounded his fist against the wall.

"Don't do that," Slade warned the man, and it was a warning with a dark, dangerous edge to it.

That danger was still in every bit of his expression when he shoved the phone into his pocket and caught onto her. "Come on. We have to leave *now*."

SLADE REMINDED HIMSELF that the kidnapper's threat could be a bluff. An out-and-out lie. But it didn't feel like a lie to his gut. There was an acid pit churning in his stomach, and he wanted to rip this man limb from limb.

And he just might.

After he rescued the baby that this bastard was using like a chess pawn.

"What'd he say to you?" Maya asked. They hurried downstairs and through the house to the back door.

Slade hated to repeat it. Hated that Maya even had to consider a possibility that was almost certainly a lie anyway. But if he didn't tell her, then her worst fears would run wild.

"He said he put out the word that he had a marshal's baby to sell on the black market, and that an old enemy, someone that I'd arrested, said he'd pay top dollar."

Maya sucked in her breath. "Is that possible? Do you have an old enemy who'd do that?"

"I've arrested a lot of scum, and yeah, they're enemies." It hurt to say that and cut him to the core that it might be true. But there was another side to this. "If we're dealing with Gambill, he'd have the contacts to get out the word about the baby, but I don't think he's had enough time for someone from my past to come back with an offer."

Slade opened the door, looked out and saw the beehive of activity. Dallas was there giving out Kevlar vests to Randall, Nadine and Chase. Ironic that one of those vests might protect the very person who'd set up these crimes. Of course, maybe the kidnapper was operating alone. If it was Gambill, he was certainly capable of something like this.

"I'm so sorry." Maya gave him a gentle kiss, and that helped more than Slade had ever expected a kiss to help.

"Let's finish this." He threw open the door and stepped into the middle of the chaos.

Nadine and Chase were bickering, but when the woman saw them, she stopped and lifted the canvas bag in the air. "I came with the money."

"And she thinks she deserves a medal for it," Chase snarled. "It's my money, and all she had to do was pick it up from the bank. When this is over, one way or another, I'm getting you out of my house and my life."

"You won't, not without paying me half of everything."

"Can we just get on with this?" Randall snapped. He, too, had a bag, and the moment Cutter led two horses out of the barn, Randall went to one and climbed into the saddle.

Chase did the same, and as if it were a chore, he pulled Nadine into the saddle behind him. Slade hadn't even thought to ask any of them if they could ride, but it didn't seem to be an issue.

Slade got on his black gelding, Wolf, which one

of the other ranch hands led out. He helped Maya on and then looked down at Dallas.

"Everything's in place," Dallas assured him. He handed Maya a gun and gave Slade another one that he tucked in the back waist of his jeans. "Wyatt and Declan are in the pasture, keeping a safe distance but ready if you need them." He pointed to the trio of barns and stables. "There are at least two men on each, including one of the deputies. We have the house covered, too."

"What about Clayton? Any word about Lenora?" Maya asked.

It surprised Slade that she could think of his brother and sister-in-law at a time like this. They'd been in the back of Slade's mind, too.

Dallas shook his head. "After you're back and this guy's behind bars, we can go to the hospital and wait for the baby to come."

An arrest was being optimistic, but Slade knew that's exactly what had to happen. No way would he let this dirt wad get away with what he'd been doing, and that threat to the baby was the last straw. This moron was going down, and he'd be the one to do it.

It was dark already, but thankfully there were enough security lights on the barns and outbuilding. A decent moon, too, so he should be able to navigate the pasture. It also helped that he knew every nook and cranny, but he also knew there were plenty of places for someone to hide and ambush them.

Chase maneuvered his horse closer to Slade's. "When the kidnapper called me, he said the baby might be your biological child. Is he?"

Maya had her arms around his waist, and her grip tightened. She was probably trying to comfort him, but they were well past that point. "Maybe."

"Yours?" Randall snapped. "How the hell did you get involved in this?"

"Long story," Slade mumbled. And it was one he didn't care to discuss with Randall.

Randall cursed and said something under his breath that Slade didn't catch. "Well, if the kid is mine, I want him."

"Why?" Chase immediately challenged. "Because Gina will come back to you if you have the baby?"

Randall didn't deny, nor did he agree. He eased the mare away from them and looked around as if he expected someone to jump out at them any moment now. That could happen, and that's why Slade kept watch, too.

"The only reason you want the baby is to irritate me," Nadine tossed out there.

"I want a child. An heir," Chase argued.

And that said it all. Again, there was no mention of love or fatherhood. Chase wanted someone to run his business after he was gone, and if he could use the child to get rid of Nadine, even better.

The two started to argue again, making it impossible for Slade to hear what was going on around them.

"Shut up, both of you," he warned them, and he didn't leave room for argument.

Good thing, too, because the moment they hushed Slade could have sworn he heard something. Not the wind, nor the cattle moving around. But something. Maybe his brothers. They were out there somewhere. So maybe he was sensing their movement. Slade hoped that was all there was to it anyway.

The cleared pasture gave way to an area with trees. Oaks and hackberries. The fence was beyond that, which meant the kidnapper had to be close.

Well, unless this was a trap.

So why hadn't the SOB called? And where was the baby? Because Slade certainly wasn't hearing any cries.

Slade reined in and motioned for the others to do the same. He cut off Nadine with a sharp glare when she started to say something. Finally, other than his heartbeat crashing in his ears, he got the quiet he needed.

Still no sounds of the kidnapper.

"What now?" Randall asked.

"We wait until he contacts us." But Slade had no

sooner said that when he finally heard something he could identify.

A footstep.

Soft and to his right.

He turned in that direction, looked around but saw nothing. But he didn't miss the sound. No way to miss that.

The bullet went blasting past him.

## Chapter Eighteen

Slade moved so fast that Maya didn't even see it coming. He hooked his arm around her waist and pulled her off the horse and to the ground. The gelding reared, the sound of the shot spooking it.

"Stay low," Slade warned her, and gripped her wrist to pull her away from the gelding with one hand and drew his gun with the other. Good thing, too, or she would have been trampled.

She managed to hang on to the gun that Dallas had given her, and Slade started running with her in tow. He didn't stop until they were behind one of the trees. Only then was Maya able to see that Randall and Chase were doing the same—but on the other side of the horses. However, Chase had left Nadine behind, and she was still trying to dismount a horse that was prancing around and ready to buck.

"Hell," Slade grumbled. "I'll have to go out there and help her."

Since that meant him going back in the open, Maya shook off his grip so that she could hold him back. She was about to launch into an argument about why that wouldn't be a good idea, but thankfully Nadine resolved it for them. She practically toppled off the horse, and while still hanging on to the money bag, she ran behind one of the trees.

"What the hell's going on?" Slade shouted.

"False alarm," the kidnapper shouted.

He was close by, but Maya couldn't see him. It was a lot darker here than in the open pasture, and the tree limbs blocked a lot of the moonlight.

"My buddy got a little trigger happy, but everything's okay now," the man added.

That gave Maya no reassurance whatsoever. Neither did the next sound she heard. A baby crying. And not just crying, either. The child started to sob. It broke her heart to think of an innocent baby in the middle of all of this, but maybe they could put a quick, safe end to it.

"You got the money?" the man shouted over the baby's cries. It was hard to pinpoint, but the sounds seemed to be coming from straight ahead, maybe even on the other side of the fence.

Not good.

Because that could mean the kidnapper would have an easier time escaping. Judging from the rock-hard muscles in Slade's body, he was going to do everything to make sure that didn't happen.

"We got the money," Slade answered. "And Maya won't be the one delivering it this time."

"Agreed."

Maya didn't know who was more surprised by that—she or Slade. She'd prepared herself to make the money drop and bring back the baby. So what had changed this time? Maybe Andrea's death had played some part in this?

"Marshal, you'll play delivery boy for this one," the kidnapper added. "And you'll do it unarmed."

Her breath stalled in her throat. Mercy. She didn't want Slade to go out there without a gun. At least if she was the one to do this, he could cover her. Then she remembered that Dallas had given him a backup weapon. Maybe the kidnapper wouldn't see it and make Slade surrender it, too.

"Randall and Chase, throw the bags out from where you're cowering," the kidnapper went on.

Neither man argued. The bags thudded against the ground in the small clearing between the clumps of trees. Slade took out his phone and fired off a text to Declan. You have eyes on us?

It only took a few seconds for Declan to respond: Not you, only the money bags.

I'm headed out there now, Slade responded. Try to watch Maya. He fired off that last text and handed her his phone.

It helped her nerves a little that Declan and Wyatt would be able to see him when he stepped out, but Maya was terrified about the stepping-out part.

Also, she wasn't too happy about Slade putting her safety ahead of his.

"Be careful," she whispered, and kissed him. Not some gentle peck. She really kissed him and prayed he'd come back safely to her.

"You, too." He lingered a moment, then glanced down at the gun she had gripped in her hand. "Use it if you need to." He dropped a kiss on her lips.

And that was it. The heart-stopping reminder and the equally heart-stopping kiss.

Slade slung the money bag over his shoulder, and with his gun ready, he stepped out from the trees. The baby's cries tapered off, making it a little easier for her to hear. But she had no idea what to listen for. Clearly, the kidnapper had some kind of backup, and it was possible those men were in the same trees where she and the others were hiding.

"First of all, drop that gun from your holster," the kidnapper shouted. "Then pick up the other bags, and keep walking toward the fence. Drop the gun," he repeated when Slade kept hold of it.

Finally, though, Slade eased the weapon to the ground just inches from him, and he pinned his attention in the direction of the kidnapper's voice, even when he stooped to retrieve the other two bags.

"Now put down the second gun," the kidnapper warned.

Slade shook his head. "I didn't bring one."

Mercy, would he believe Slade?

Maya was breathing through her mouth now, and her heart was beating way too fast. She had no hope of correcting either, and she certainly wouldn't relax until this was over and both Slade and the baby were safe.

"Start walking," the man demanded.

Slade did, and Maya felt each step with a thud of her heart. She felt the relief, too. Well, just a little. At least Slade had that second gun to protect himself. This had to end.

"When you get to the fence," the kidnapper added, "drop the money bags onto the other side."

Slade stopped and shook his head. "Give me the baby first. Then you get the money."

The man didn't answer, and Maya held her breath again. Waiting and praying. When the pain shot through her hand, she realized she had a death grip on the gun, and she loosened her fingers a little.

"How do I know you won't take the kid and the money and run?" the man countered.

"How do I know you won't do the same?" Slade fired back.

The silence came again. Even the baby had stopped crying. And the moments crawled by.

"All right," the kidnapper finally said. "Come to the fence, and I'll hand you the kid at the same moment you hand me the money."

Slade started to walk again, and soon—too soon—Maya could no longer see him unless she leaned out from the tree. Something she was sure Slade wouldn't want her to do. Plus, doing that might obstruct the view that Declan and Wyatt had of him.

She waited again. Until she heard a strange sound. Movement maybe to what would be Slade's right. And it was just the beginning. Suddenly, there were a lot of sounds. Footsteps. Leaves rustling. Even whispers.

Each new sound made her heart race even faster.

She didn't want to call out to Slade, but she had to see what was going on. Maya peeked out from the tree and saw something she didn't want to see.

Her heart went to her knees.

Because, cursing, Slade dived back behind one of the trees near the fence.

"What the hell's going on?" Slade called out.

"Not sure." The kidnapper's voice seemed strained. Definitely not his usual cocky demeanor.

And before Maya could figure out what was happening, the bullets started to fly.

SLADE DREW THE gun from the back waist of his jeans.

All hell was breaking loose. The bullets were flying everywhere, Nadine was screaming at the top of her lungs, and the kidnapper was spewing profanity. Slade tuned that out because he had to do something to stop those shots.

"Stay down, Maya, all the way down on the ground!" he yelled, and he hoped like the devil that she'd listen. The others, too. Slade definitely didn't want Randall or the Colliers in on this.

Whatever *this* was.

One second all seemed to be going as well as it could be going. He'd spotted the ski-mask wearing kidnapper on the other side of the fence, and just as the idiot had said, he had the baby in his arms. Slade had been just seconds away from the exchange when everything turned bad.

The kidnapper had blurted out some profanity and had suddenly dropped to the ground. A second later the bullets started flying. Now the question was why? Obviously, this wasn't part of the kidnapper's plan, but then, things had gone wrong with the last money exchange, too.

Slade looked out at the clearing, at the moonlight glinting off his gun, but there was no one in his line of sight. Definitely no shooter.

"Who's taking shots at us?" Slade asked to no one in particular.

But it was the kidnapper who answered. "I'm figuring your brothers."

"Not a chance." They wouldn't risk one of those bullets hitting the baby.

"It's not Declan or Wyatt firing the shots," Maya called out. "I just got a text from them, and they want to know what's going on."

*Welcome to the club.* "Nadine? Stop screaming and tell me what's going on where you are."

"I'm not sure," she shouted through the sobs and over the blasts of the bullets. "Chase isn't here. He ran off before the shots started."

That wasn't a good sign, and it could mean Chase was the one doing the shooting. But why? Why would he risk hurting a child he seemed to want?

He could be faking that want, that's why.

Or he could know the baby was safe. Maybe the kidnapper had ducked behind some kind of barrier that he'd put in place before this meeting. Of course, that didn't answer the biggest question of all.

Why would anyone fire shots in the middle of a ransom drop?

"Randall?" Slade called out. He wanted everyone accounted for, but Randall didn't answer.

Slade tried again.

Still no answer.

It was possible that Randall had been shot. There were certainly enough bullets for that to happen, or like Chase, he could be the one shooting.

Or even Nadine.

Slade didn't trust any of them.

He lifted his head a fraction so he could try to pinpoint the direction of the shots, but just like that, they stopped. He waited, the seconds ticking off in his head, but he didn't hear any movement. The baby was a different story. He was crying, and judging from the sound, he was still on the other side of the fence with the kidnapper. So the guy hadn't run after all.

But he likely would run now that the shots had stopped.

"Your money's out here with me," Slade reminded the guy.

"I know." And that's all the kidnapper said for several moments. "Did you see who fired those shots?"

"No. How about your hired guns? Did they see?"

"No."

Whether that was true or not, Slade didn't know. Didn't care at this point. He just wanted to make the transfer so he could get the baby to safety. Because once he had the child, Declan and Wyatt could move in and help him get Maya out of there.

"Declan still doesn't see anyone," Maya relayed.

But his brother would continue to look. That was the advantage of having family as backup. Both Wyatt and Declan would do whatever it took to make this drop work.

"I'm crawling to the edge of the fence right by that scrawny hackberry," the kidnapper said. "Meet me there with the money."

"Be careful," Maya repeated. And he heard the fear and worry in her voice. There wasn't much Slade could do to make it go away except finish this as fast as he could.

Slade started crawling, and he tried to keep his gun hidden behind the trio of money bags. He heard the movement on the other side of the fence. Exactly where it should be if the kidnapper was going through with this deal.

When Slade made it to the last tree before the fence, he stopped and stood so he could be in a better position to react. He leaned out, looked around.

And spotted the guy.

He was dressed in dark clothes and still wearing the ski mask. The night almost completely camouflaged him, but there was just enough light for Slade to see the gun the guy was holding. He was also nervous. He kept moving his head around, and he looked ready to bolt.

However, what Slade didn't see was the baby.

"Where is he?" Slade demanded.

The guy tipped his head just to his left. "He's in his carrier. All safe and sound."

The baby's cries confirmed the location but not the safe-and-sound part.

"Now toss over the money," he demanded.

"Not until I have the baby."

"You can climb over the fence and get him as soon as I'm out of here."

There was something different in the guy's voice. An urgency no doubt caused by the shots that'd been fired. He glanced around again. Cursed. And then pointed his gun directly at Slade.

"Sorry," he said to Slade, "but I got my orders, and you're to die."

Slade had figured it'd come down to this. He already had his backup weapon in place, and he took full advantage of that. He didn't aim for the guy's chest. The Kevlar would save him, and heaven knows what this guy would do to the baby then.

No. It was a risk Slade couldn't take.

Slade saw the man's hand tense. Ready to fire. But Slade fired first.

Two shots to the head.

A strangled sound ripped from the man's throat, and he dropped to the ground.

"Slade?" Maya shouted.

"I'm okay." Well, maybe. He had to get to the baby, and he was pretty sure the kidnapper had a comrade stashed out there somewhere. After all, someone had fired those shots.

Slade dropped the money bags and vaulted across the fence. He heard the footstep. Just one. And he pivoted in that direction. He caught just a glimpse of the second gunman. Also dressed in black and wearing a ski mask. Slade took aim. Fired and finished him off.

He didn't take the time to unmask either of the men, but he checked to make sure they were dead. They were. Then he hurried to the baby. He wasn't hard to find—Slade just followed his cries. With the sorry luck Maya and he'd been having, Slade halfway expected to see a recording device playing the baby's cries.

But it was the real deal.

The baby was in a carrier seat similar to Evan's, and the kidnapper had positioned it in the center of some limestone boulders. The baby was nestled down in there deep so that he'd be protected from the bullets. That was something at least. The kidnapper had taken some measures to keep the baby safe.

Keeping his gun ready, Slade lifted the seat and glanced down at the baby. He didn't want to think about this possibly being his child. Didn't want to think of anything but getting him to safety.

Slade hurried back to the fence and climbed over. Still using the trees as cover, he opened his mouth to call out to his brothers so they could move in to help.

But Slade heard a sound that he definitely didn't want to hear. Not a gunshot this time. Something worse.

Maya's scream tore through the silence.

## Chapter Nineteen

Maya heard the movement behind her a split second too late. She whirled around, her gun ready, but something knocked it from her hand.

Not *something,* she amended.

*Someone.*

She couldn't see who it was, but she definitely felt the blow to the back of her head. The pain exploded through her brain, and even though she tried to catch on to anything to break her fall, she didn't manage it. She dropped straight to the ground.

The fall didn't help. It knocked what little breath she had out of her, and before she could recover and try to figure out what was happening to her, someone latched on to her hair and dragged her back to her feet.

"Maya?" Slade yelled.

He'd no doubt heard her scream, and Maya tried to do it again so he'd know where she was, but she rethought that. Someone had fired those shots, and since Slade was alive, she didn't want him walking into an ambush.

She tried to fight. Hard to do with no breath and the pain stabbing through her head.

Mercy, how badly was she hurt?

Had the person managed to give her a concussion? Or worse? Maya tried not to think of the "worse" part, and she started flailing her arms around, trying to make contact with anything that would get her attacker to release her.

She failed.

The grip on her hair got tighter, and Maya found herself being slammed against someone's chest.

A man.

That barely had time to register when she felt something else add to the pain. Not a gun. But a knife.

Oh, God.

He had a knife.

A thousand flashbacks came. The worst of the worst. They tore through her right along with the pain from the blow to the back of the head. And she relived every slice from the blade that had nearly left her dead all those years ago.

"Maya!" Slade again.

She felt herself go limp, and all the fight left her. Maya couldn't make herself move. Couldn't breathe. Couldn't scream.

Not even when she felt the tip of the knife flick against her throat.

She was going to die. Right here. Right now. He would finish what her ex had started. Maya drew in the last breath she figured she'd ever take.

And then she thought of Evan.

Slade, too.

They were both there, right along with the brutal images of the attack.

Everything inside her went still. An eerie calmness that seemed to reach right down into her soul. But in that calmness, she knew one thing. She had to fight to stay alive not just for herself but for Slade and her baby.

She forced herself to breathe. Relaxed her throat. And focused. Maya gathered every bit of her strength and rammed her elbow into her attacker's stomach. It was risky. He could just cut her throat, but her will to live was the only weapon she had. He staggered back just a fraction, but before she could start running, he latched on to her again.

"Don't make me kill you here," he snarled.

Maya knew that voice, but before she could say his name, Slade came running into the small clearing where she was. He had a baby carrier in his left hand. His gun ready in his right. But obviously he wasn't in a position to fight back, not with the baby in the middle of this.

"Let her go, Randall," Slade ordered.

Even in the darkness, she could see the intense expression on his face. Could hear it in his voice. He would do anything humanly possible to save her, but it might not be enough.

With the knife still at her throat, Randall shook his head and mumbled something. At first Maya thought he was talking to her, but it took her a moment to realize he was speaking into a small communicator that he had in his ear.

"Move in closer," Randall said to the person on the other end of that device. "Let me know when you're in place, and we can get this show on the road—literally."

He was talking to his henchman, no doubt. But what did he want with her? He'd certainly had a chance to kill her and he hadn't taken it.

"My brothers are out there," Slade warned him. "They won't let you get away. *I* won't let you get away," he added through clenched teeth.

"Getting away isn't what I have in mind." Unlike Slade's, Randall's voice was actually calm. Too calm, maybe. "Now that you've killed Gambill and his friend, I have no choice but to use Maya."

So Gambill had been the one behind the mask. That didn't surprise her, but she was shocked to hear that he was dead. And his backup, too. Slade had almost certainly been the one to eliminate them, and despite that it meant two men had died, Maya had no sympathy for them.

Or for Randall.

They'd endangered the lives of those two babies they'd kidnapped, and Andrea was dead. For that matter, Chase and Nadine might be dead, as well.

"Did you kill the Colliers?" Maya asked.

"Not yet. My assistant is holding them at gunpoint so they won't be tempted to help you. I don't want any interference, and I want to make this short and sweet."

"What the hell does that mean?" Slade snapped.

The baby stirred in the carrier, but Slade only turned it so that the child wasn't facing Randall. The carrier wouldn't protect the child if shots were fired, so Maya prayed that his brothers would be there soon.

"Well, the plan was for you to be dead," Randall said, his attention nailed to Slade, "and for Gambill to use the kid there to force Maya to have Evan's DNA tested. Best-laid plans went south again just like at the barn. Gambill set off those damn rifles before I could tell Maya what I needed her to do. After Andrea was shot—an accident, I promise— I had to regroup."

Maya hated to hear the details. Each one made the flashbacks worse. Of course, the knife at her throat didn't help, either, but the worst was having Slade and the baby there in danger.

"Why do you want Evan's DNA?" Slade asked.

"It's obvious, isn't it? If he's my son, then I need

to take him. Gina will listen to reason if I have the kid. Even though she gave him up for adoption, she won't want me to raise him without her being around to, well, supervise."

So this was a crazy form of blackmail to get Gina back. One that might work if Gina knew just how dangerous Randall truly was.

"What if she didn't give him up?" Maya had to do or say whatever it took to give Slade's brothers a chance to stop this. Besides, she might be able to talk Randall out of whatever he was planning. "What if she let you believe she gave him up and then disappeared with the child?"

"Then I'll find her." His voice was no longer calm, and it was laced with emotions she was all too familiar with. Obsession and violence.

A dangerous combination.

"You obviously don't care a thing about your son," Maya tossed at him. "Because if Evan's your son, you could have hurt him when you had your hired gun ram the SUV into my car."

"That wasn't supposed to happen. It was supposed to be a quick smash-and-grab, but when I found out what the idiot had done, he paid for it."

With his life. So Randall had killed him. That was one mystery solved, but Maya hadn't needed to hear it to know he was capable of murder.

"You said this was my son," Slade reminded him, but he also shifted his position and eased the carrier onto the ground. Maybe freeing up his hands for a fight that Maya was certain he wouldn't want to have with the baby so close and the knife at her throat.

"He might be. He sure isn't mine," Randall insisted. "I just got back the DNA results."

"So you lied." Slade shifted again. Inching closer.

"It's only a lie if it turns out to be one. In fact, I wouldn't have even known you were in this DNA lottery if I hadn't been checking for labs running DNA tests on the babies. After a few bribes, I learned the kids' DNA was being compared to yours. Wasn't hard to figure out that you were looking for your kid."

Without warning, Randall jabbed the end of the knife against her neck, cutting into the skin. "Keep moving, Marshal, and the next cut will be a lot deeper."

Slade stopped, and his gaze met hers. He didn't say anything, not with his mouth anyway, but she could almost hear him say he was sorry. This wasn't his fault. He was as much of a victim as the babies, the Rands, Andrea and she were. But he would put this on his shoulders and bear the weight of it.

"We need to end this now," Randall insisted.

"Why the hurry?" Slade tossed back. "You had ample opportunity to kidnap Maya while we were at the safe house after you had someone plant the tracking device in the grocery sack. Yet you waited for hours."

Randall cursed, and she felt the muscles tense in his hand. "I had to regroup then, too. The woman I hired to watch the kids ran out on me, and I had to find someone else."

Maya cringed at the thought of those babies being at the mercy of this monster, but at least Caleb was safe now.

"Good," Randall said into the communicator. He looked at Slade again. "My gunman has your brothers in his sight. Tell them to stay put. Do it now!" he yelled when Slade didn't say anything.

"Randall says his gunman has you in his sight," Slade finally shouted. What Declan and Wyatt would do with that info she didn't know, but Maya prayed they could still help.

"And now we have to get moving," Randall continued. "This is how it'll work. My second assistant will collect the money bags. I need it to pay for this whole kidnapping operation, and then Maya and I will go back to the house. If she makes one wrong move, I'll cut her. It might not kill her, but she'll wish it had. And once we're at the house, I'll get the DNA sample from the kid."

"Then what?" Maya was surprised Slade could speak with his jaw clenched that way.

"Maya and Evan will have to stay with me for a few days. Just until I have the DNA results. If

Evan's mine, then I take him. If he's not, then I'll give him back."

She knew it wouldn't be that easy. No. Randall would have to kill her because she was a witness. Slade, too. And that also meant he'd likely given his henchmen orders to kill Slade's brothers and the Colliers.

Maya was afraid to move, but she was more terrified of losing Slade and her son. She wasn't sure what she should do until she heard the scream bubble up in her throat. Her yell blasted through the night.

Randall cursed and moved. No doubt to jab the knife into her, but Maya twisted around, trying to break free.

From the corner of her eye, she saw the movement. A whirl of motion. Slade came right at them, and he shoved her aside as if she weighed nothing. Maya landed on the ground, and Slade rammed right into Randall.

The men went flying.

Oh, God. The knife.

The moonlight hit the blade just right, and she saw Randall swing it at Slade. He was trying to kill him.

Maya didn't have a gun. Randall had knocked hers somewhere on the ground, and it might do more harm than good if she jumped into the middle of the fight.

It was a horrible thing to watch. The life-and-death battle going on right in front of her. She felt around on the ground, feeling for anything she could use, and she found some rocks. It wasn't much, but when Randall rolled on top of Slade, Maya threw the rocks, pelting him in the back.

Randall cursed. It was vicious. As was the look on his face when he whirled around, ready to launch himself at her.

But Slade didn't let that happen.

He grabbed Randall by the back of the neck, turned and body-slammed him face first into the ground. Even though it must have broken a bone or two, Randall came up fighting. Like a crazed killer.

Slade punched him with his left fist, and Randall's head flopped back. He tried to get up again, but this time Slade put his gun right in the center of Randall's forehead.

"Move, *please,*" Slade growled. "Because I'm looking for an excuse to send you straight to hell."

Randall stopped fighting.

But Maya held her breath. Waiting. Praying this was over. However, she wasn't sure it truly was until she heard the footsteps. She raced to the baby, using her body to shield him just in case this was Randall's henchman.

But it was Declan and Wyatt.

Declan hurried to Slade and hauled Randall to

his feet. He took some plastic cuffs from his pocket and restrained the man.

"Are you okay?" Slade asked her, his words rushing out with his breath. "Did he hurt you?"

Maya put her fingers over the trickle of blood running down her neck. It hurt, but she doubted it was serious. Still, Slade cursed and then cursed Randall. Since she was afraid Slade would beat the man to death, she pulled him away.

"I'm fine." That was a lie. Her nerves were a wreck, and she didn't think she'd stop shaking anytime soon.

"Is he okay?" Wyatt asked, looking over her at the baby.

Maya had to see for herself. She didn't know how the baby managed it, but he was still sound asleep. The relief flooded through her.

Well, some relief.

Maya scooped up the carrier and hurried to Slade. Even though they had an audience, she rushed toward him. However, before she could put her arm around him, Slade's attention went to Wyatt.

"How many of Randall's men did you find?" he asked Wyatt.

"Just one. He was holding the Colliers at gunpoint."

Randall laughed, and the sound nearly froze her blood.

Slade cursed and pulled out his phone. "Cutter," he said the second his ranch hand answered. "There's another gunman out there, and he's probably heading to the ranch. Stop him before he can take Evan."

## Chapter Twenty

Slade couldn't move fast enough, but thankfully everyone was cooperating.

Maya grabbed the baby and the carrier, and they hurried back to the horses. They had to get back to the ranch because he couldn't risk someone kidnapping Evan.

From the corner of his eye he saw Nadine and Chase. They were arguing, and Chase drew back his hand and slapped her hard. Under normal circumstances, Slade would have intervened, but this was far from normal.

"Arrest them both first chance you get," Slade said to Wyatt and Declan, who were leading Randall back in the direction of the ranch. They couldn't risk putting him on horseback in case he did something to make the horse throw them and escaped. So it wouldn't be a fast journey.

"Call Dallas," Slade said, handing Maya his phone. There wasn't much room in the saddle with both of them and the baby, but she managed to take hold, and she found Dallas's number in his contacts.

"Randall could have a gunman coming to the house," she relayed.

And Slade held his breath, praying the gunman wasn't already there.

"It's under control," Slade heard Dallas say. Maya had put the call on speaker. "We've got the gunman, and the house is secure. The ranch hands are out now looking for anyone else that Randall might have managed to get on the grounds, but there haven't been any other security sensors triggered."

Slade didn't know whose sound of relief was louder, his or Maya's. She dropped her head on the back of his shoulder and mumbled a prayer of thanks. Slade added one of his own.

But they weren't out of the woods yet.

Now that he could slow down, he looked back at her and tried to see how bad her injury was. In the moonlight the streak of blood looked black, but he knew what it was. And it made him want to kill Randall. The acid churned in his stomach at the thought of that bastard putting his hands on Maya.

"Maya needs to go to the hospital," Slade told Dallas. "Randall…cut her." He nearly choked on the words. "And we should have the baby checked out, too.

"Dr. Landry's still here. I didn't want her outside the house with the gunmen at large."

Good. The sooner Maya and the baby were attended to, the better. Slade ended the call and rode toward the ranch.

"The baby is Will Collier," Maya said, easing off his cap so she could look at his hair.

So that meant both missing babies were accounted for. That alone was a miracle. Usually these kinds of cases didn't have happy endings, and here they'd gotten two of them.

And maybe a third.

Because either this baby or Evan could be his son.

Slade took his phone from Maya and called Dallas back. "Randall said he did DNA tests on the babies. Can you track them down and compare the DNA to mine?"

Dallas didn't hesitate. "I'll get right on it."

The ride seemed to take an eternity, but Slade finally saw the lights of the back porch. Even though the threat was over, he couldn't wait to get inside. The moment he reined in, he helped Maya out of the saddle, took the carrier and rushed her into the kitchen.

His attention went right to her neck.

He didn't curse, because there was a roomful of people in the den just off the kitchen. His brothers, sister-in-law, Caitlyn, Stella, who was holding a sleeping Evan, Dr. Landry and the Rands, who were thanking everyone and preparing to leave. They looked eager to get the heck out of there, and Slade didn't blame them. Their lives had been a living hell for the past two days, and they probably wanted to get back to something normal.

Both Dallas and Harlan were on their phones, huddled in the corners of the room. Slade knew that Dallas was working on the DNA tests, and Harlan was no doubt doing mop-up on the dead gunmen and the investigation.

"Evan." Maya made a beeline for him and pulled him into her arms.

"Before he started making some calls, Dallas said you had an injury." Dr. Landry went closer to Maya and started the examination.

"Is she okay?" Slade asked the doc.

"I'm fine," Maya repeated. "But make sure the baby's all right."

Dr. Landry nodded and glanced at the baby. Slade glanced at him, too, and the baby's eyes were wide open now. He was looking around the room as if trying to figure out what the heck was going on.

"He looks pretty healthy to me," the doctor concluded, and she took some supplies from her bag. "Let me just get this wound cleaned first. Don't think stitches are necessary, but I don't want it getting infected." She dabbed away the blood, smeared on some cream she took from her bag and put a bandage over it.

"The baby's yours?" Wyatt asked, looking in the carrier seat at Will.

"Maybe." Slade glanced at Maya. "What if he is?"

The moment the doctor was finished with the bandage, Maya brushed a kiss on Slade's cheek. "Then I'm sure you'll have no trouble stopping the Colliers' adoption and taking custody of him."

Yes on both counts. The Colliers didn't deserve to have a baby.

"How's Lenora doing?" Maya asked, but she had her attention on Will as the doctor took the baby from the carrier and sat on the sofa to examine him.

"It shouldn't be much longer," Stella answered. "Clayton said he'd call as soon as the baby came." She strolled closer, watching Will.

So did the others.

Especially Slade.

He kept volleying his attention from Maya to Evan to Will.

"Got good news," Harlan said when he finished a phone call. "We found Gina, Randall's ex. She's been in hiding because she was scared of him."

Not a surprise. "So is Will her baby?" Slade asked.

Harlan shook his head. "Gina didn't give up her child. She faked the adoption to throw Randall off her trail. I'm guessing she had no idea what kind of hell it'd create."

*Hell* was a good word for it. But there was a flip side to all of this. If it hadn't been for the hell, he wouldn't have met Maya. Maybe not Evan, either.

And even though he didn't want to go back through that, he would go through worse if it meant keeping Maya.

Slade froze.

Mentally repeated that.

And suddenly everything became crystal clear. He knew exactly what he had to do.

With everyone's attention still on Will and his examination, Slade slipped his arm around Maya's waist. "I want you to marry me." He shook his head, mumbled some profanity. That sounded like an order. "Will you marry me?"

Maya blinked. Twice. "Uh, shouldn't you wait until you know if Evan is your son?"

"No. Because it doesn't matter if he is or not." Heck, that didn't sound right, either. "I mean, he already feels like my son, so it won't matter if we have the same DNA. He's my son, and I want you to be my wife. Marry me," he repeated.

She stared at him. Licked her lips. Then pushed her hair from her face. "I'll only marry you for love."

Oh. That. Well, heck. He was really putting the cart before the horse. "Easy fix. I love you."

Of course, that didn't mean she felt the same, and Slade held his breath, waiting, hoping and praying that he'd hear the answer he wanted.

Her smile said it all.

And the way she slid her hand around the back

of his neck and pulled him closer for a kiss. "I love you, too," she said against his mouth.

Instant relief. Instant heat, too, and Slade deepened the kiss until he remembered where they were. And who was watching. His brothers. His sister-in-law, Harlan's fiancée, the doctor and Stella. All seemed amused.

Even Will was watching them.

The baby was still on the doctor's lap, but he looked up at them. His expression was so intense that it made Slade smile. He picked him up and brushed a kiss on his cheek. Slade was about to press Maya for an answer, but both the doctor's and Stella's phones buzzed.

Slade held his breath, praying this wasn't another dose of bad news, but then he saw both the doctor and Stella smiling.

"Lenora just delivered a baby boy," Stella announced. "Jacob Kirby Caldwell. From the sound of it, he's got a good pair of lungs on him."

"Seven pounds, six ounces," the doctor supplied. "Just got a text from one of the nurses. Both the mom and baby are doing great."

That created a flurry of excitement. His brother had a son. The next generation for Kirby's boys.

Except it wasn't the first, Slade realized, because his son was already six weeks old.

"I'm leaving now," the doctor said. "And I expect an invitation to the wedding. If there is one." She looked at Joelle. "And maybe you'll have a girl. To balance out all this testosterone."

"I'll see what I can do," Joelle said, smiling.

The doctor headed out, and only then did Slade remember that Maya hadn't answered his proposal. She'd said the "I love you" part. He had, too, but he needed the yes.

"Don't say no," Slade insisted.

The corner of Maya's mouth lifted. "Wouldn't dream of it. You're everything I've always wanted, Slade Becker."

Declan groaned. "Not another wedding." But he winked at her.

The others came forward, each hugging Maya and congratulating him. Though it was clear they were all happy for him, no one looked ready to linger. Probably because they figured Maya and he might like a moment alone.

And Slade did.

But he knew the moment would have to wait when Dallas finished his call. Judging from his expression, he had news, but Slade couldn't tell if it was good or bad.

"Evan's not your biological son," Dallas started. "His birth mother is the person on his adoption records, and she voluntarily gave him up. Nothing fishy about the adoption."

"And what about Will?" Slade hadn't intended to hold his breath, but that's exactly what happened.

Dallas nodded. "He's yours."

The emotions slammed through him. The shock. The sheer happiness. Everything. Until Slade remembered they were dealing with Randall. "Could Randall have faked the tests?"

"He didn't. The results match the ones that Declan ran for both babies. Will is your son."

Another slam, but the strongest one of all was the love. It filled every inch of him, and Slade knew it was a love he didn't want to let go of.

Dallas left with the others, and later Slade would thank them for that.

Because he couldn't hold back any longer, Slade kissed Maya. It wasn't easy to do since they were both holding babies.

Their sons.

"You okay with this?" Slade asked.

She smiled, and he could taste that smile in their next kiss. "Better than okay. I get a smokin'-hot husband and two sons. I'm the luckiest person on earth."

No. Slade had that honor. He had Evan, Will and Maya. For the first time in his life, he had something he'd never really had.

A family of his own.

\* \* \* \* \*

*USA TODAY bestselling author
Delores Fossen's miniseries*
THE MARSHALS OF MAVERICK COUNTY
*continues next month with
JUSTICE IS COMING.
Look for it wherever
Harlequin Intrigue books are sold!*

# LARGER-PRINT BOOKS!
## GET 2 FREE LARGER-PRINT NOVELS PLUS
## 2 FREE GIFTS!

**H HARLEQUIN®**

# INTRIGUE®

## BREATHTAKING ROMANTIC SUSPENSE

HILP13R

# LARGER-PRINT BOOKS!

## GET 2 FREE
## LARGER-PRINT NOVELS
## PLUS 2 FREE
## MYSTERY GIFTS

Love Inspired
## SUSPENSE
RIVETING INSPIRATIONAL ROMANCE

### Larger-print novels are now available...

**YES!** Please send me 2 FREE LARGER-PRINT Love Inspired® Suspense novels and my 2 FREE mystery gifts (gifts are worth about $10). After receiving them, if I don't wish to receive any more books, I can return the shipping statement marked "cancel." If I don't cancel, I will receive 4 brand-new novels every month and be billed just $5.24 per book in the U.S. or $5.74 per book in Canada. That's a savings of at least 23% off the cover price. It's quite a bargain! Shipping and handling is just 50¢ per book in the U.S. and 75¢ per book in Canada.* I understand that accepting the 2 free books and gifts places me under no obligation to buy anything. I can always return a shipment and cancel at any time. Even if I never buy another book, the two free books and gifts are mine to keep forever.

110/310 IDN F5CC

| Name | (PLEASE PRINT) | |
|---|---|---|

| Address | | Apt. # |
|---|---|---|

| City | State/Prov. | Zip/Postal Code |
|---|---|---|

Signature (if under 18, a parent or guardian must sign)

### Mail to the Harlequin® Reader Service:
**IN U.S.A.:** P.O. Box 1867, Buffalo, NY 14240-1867
**IN CANADA:** P.O. Box 609, Fort Erie, Ontario L2A 5X3

**Are you a current subscriber to Love Inspired Suspense books and want to receive the larger-print edition?**
**Call 1-800-873-8635 or visit www.ReaderService.com.**

\* Terms and prices subject to change without notice. Prices do not include applicable taxes. Sales tax applicable in N.Y. Canadian residents will be charged applicable taxes. Offer not valid in Quebec. This offer is limited to one order per household. Not valid for current subscribers to Love Inspired Suspense larger-print books. All orders subject to credit approval. Credit or debit balances in a customer's account(s) may be offset by any other outstanding balance owed by or to the customer. Please allow 4 to 6 weeks for delivery. Offer available while quantities last.

**Your Privacy**—The Harlequin® Reader Service is committed to protecting your privacy. Our Privacy Policy is available online at www.ReaderService.com or upon request from the Harlequin Reader Service.

We make a portion of our mailing list available to reputable third parties that offer products we believe may interest you. If you prefer that we not exchange your name with third parties, or if you wish to clarify or modify your communication preferences, please visit us at www.ReaderService.com/consumerschoice or write to us at Harlequin Reader Service Preference Service, P.O. Box 9062, Buffalo, NY 14269. Include your complete name and address.

LISLPDIR13R

# *Reader Service*.com

## Manage your account online!
- Review your order history
- Manage your payments
- Update your address

> *We've designed
> the Harlequin® Reader Service
> website just for you.*

## Enjoy all the features!
- Reader excerpts from any series
- Respond to mailings and
  special monthly offers
- Discover new series available to you
- Browse the Bonus Bucks catalog
- Share your feedback

*Visit us at:*
## ReaderService.com